Why couldn't Pa show his disappointment like any other human being?

George took a step forward. "Pa," he called softly.

"What is it now?"

George wanted to ask if they had done everything they could to save Ugly Cow and her calf. He wanted to hear Pa say that, yes, when he had been twelve years old, he felt just as shaken, just as queasy.

"Speak up, will you?" Pa asked impatiently.

"Nothing," George mumbled. He beat a hasty retreat to the pump. What good would talking do? After all, Pa never admitted that he was uncertain.

The bitter fact was that, unlike Pa, he felt no sense of accomplishment from farm work. That was the difference between farming and music. When George played a piece on his trombone, there was a beginning, a middle, and an end. He had created something—a melody. But when he worked on the farm, he just seemed to do the same hard, dirty, dull chores over and over again. Nothing was ever really finished. And what was the point?

George pulled off his mud- and straw-caked boots and flung them angrily outside the soddy door. He would never follow in his father's footsteps. Never.

George
On His Own

Laurie Lawlor

Illustrated by Toby Gowing

A MINSTREL® BOOK

Published by POCKET BOOKS
New York   London   Toronto   Sydney   Tokyo   Singapore

Books by Laurie Lawlor

The Worm Club
How to Survive the Third Grade
Addie Across the Prairie
Addie's Long Summer
Addie's Dakota Winter
George on His Own
Heartland: Come Away with Me

Available from MINSTREL Books

A Minstrel Book published by
POCKET BOOKS, a division of Simon & Schuster Inc.
1230 Avenue of the Americas, New York, NY 10020

ISBN: 0-671-52608-1

First Minstrel Books printing June 1996

10 9 8 7 6 5 4 3 2 1

A MINSTREL BOOK and colophon are registered trademarks of
Simon & Schuster Inc.

Cover art by Diane Sivavec

Printed in the U.S.A.

The lines on page 59 are from the beginning of Act III, Scene 2 of *King Lear* by William Shakespeare.

CONTENTS

For my grandmother, who read my poetry,
Maria Charlotta Nelson Thompson. L.L.

1 TROMBONE DREAM

Around the edges of shrunken snow drifts, dead grass lay matted like hair trapped too long beneath a tight woolen cap. Fog shrouded the prairie. The late March morning felt cold as winter. And yet something had changed.

Restlessly, George shifted the lumpy burlap sack to his other shoulder and sniffed. The air was filled with a faint, rich earthy odor, a dizzy promise. Nowhere had he seen one bud, one green sprout, one blossom, but he knew. Spring was coming. Yes.

He cocked his head and listened. What was that half-forgotten noise? Now cradling the sack in his arms, he hurried across the empty pasture to the cutbank. He peered down. Melting snow water babbled through the slough. Soon torrents and streams would be rushing in countless swales and dry runs and ditches that were just waiting to be explored.

George whooped with delight. How deep was the slough? He had to find out.

He set the sack on dry ground and slipped off his cumbersome wool coat. After rolling up his pant leg a few inches, he lowered one foot into the swirling current. Deep, deeper yet, the numbing water went—past his ankle, his calf, his knee. Did he dare stand one-legged? If he lost his balance, he'd fall in. And what would Mother say if he again came home with his clothes soaked?

He didn't care. The risk was part of the thrill.

Holding his breath, he stood. Five seconds. Ten seconds. Fifteen seconds. When he could bear the cold no longer, he triumphantly hoisted himself back to shore and dumped water from his boot. As he wrung out his soggy pant leg, he gazed at his reflection in a puddle and imagined he was no longer twelve years old. He was all grown-up, tall and handsome, rich and famous. His unruly brown thatch was slick and parted. His freckles had disappeared. He sported a fine, dark moustache that curled up at the ends.

Inspired, he opened the sack and slipped out something shining and wondrous—a trombone. He lifted the gleaming brass instrument to his lips. The melody he played soared and plunged, as hopeful and impatient as his longing for spring. He closed his eyes and pretended he was performing a solo in a fancy, crowded San Francisco concert hall.

The audience stood up and cheered. And why not? George was the best trombone player in the world.

He smiled, then carefully replaced the instrument in the sack. From his back pocket he removed the letter he had written to his thirteen-year-old sister:

March 30, 1887

Dear Addie,

Have you gotten over the blewes yet? Only two months until you get to come home and you don't have to go back to hi school again until fall! I herd Yankton has one of those brandnew palaces where you can rolersckate indoors on a big wood floor and theirs a reel orcestra. You should go and have some fun instead of studiing so much.

The good news is that our school has been canceled because of meesles. That's fine with me.

Nellie is shure cantanckerous! Burt and Lew get along as bad as ever. Mother says I need new overalls since I grew so much.

I've been practicing every week in the Defiance Brass Band. Mr. Swain Finch lent me the trombone for free—that's the only reason Pa lets me play. Mr. Finch says I have perfect pitch, which means I can hear exactly where to slide the trombone to find just the right note.

I have a serrprize! Remember how me and Shy Fairchild have been saving money? I bet Shy

9

*and I collected more than ten tons of old bufalo
bones we found on the prarie. We got 13 dollers
from the bone man in town, who sends the bones
East to be made into fertilizer. We used strong
horse-hair snares and caught 60 dozen goffers.
The farmers think there pests but I don't think
there so bad, since each string of a dozen tales
got us 50 sents at the dry goods store. We had
$42.31. We were rich!*

*Shy ordered a repeeting rifle from the Mont-
gomery Ward catalog. Pa told me I shood buy
something practical, like a saddle horse. But I got
something better, only I won't tell you till you get
home.*

George took a pencil stub from his pocket, licked the
end, and signed his name with a flourish:

*Sincerely,
George Sydney Mills*

It took all the willpower he could muster not to tell
her everything. Nobody knew his secret—not even Shy,
his best friend since school began a year ago. George
had not told a soul because he was afraid of what his
parents would do if they found out that he used all the
money he had earned to buy the borrowed trombone from
Mr. Finch. Just thinking that the trombone was his to

10

keep forever made him feel like jumping and hollering and kicking his heels together!

This was his plan: as soon as Addie returned from Yankton, where she was boarding while attending her first year of high school, he would make an announcement in front of the whole family. He'd tell them all he had purchased the trombone. Addie would be so impressed that she would help convince Pa and Mother he'd done the right thing.

Addie was always interested in how George's music studies were coming along. She'd written to him about a real concert she had attended, where the performers wore band uniforms with gold braid and visored caps. She said George would look very fine in such an outfit.

When Addie had come home at Christmas, George noticed the special, grown-up way she was treated by Pa and Mother. Was that because she had seen something of the wide world beyond Hutchinson County? His parents listened politely to her new opinions about how women ought to have the right to vote and how liquor was the cause of all evil in the world. After she went back to school, the only subject Pa and Mother ever seemed to talk about was Addie, Addie, Addie. "Your sister is the first Mills to ever graduate from grammar school. She won the only high school scholarship in Hutchinson County," Pa reminded George almost daily. "Getting a teaching certificate is a practical way for her to get ahead in the world."

Getting ahead in the world seemed very important to Pa. He had already decided how his two eldest children would succeed. Addie was to be a scholar. But George's unremarkable school performance meant that he must stay on the farm to make his mark.

George scowled. It was true that he hated school. He could read all right, but he had no head for spelling or numbers. He planned that just as soon as he passed eighth grade, he would never enter another deathly boring schoolroom the rest of his life. As for Pa's idea about George staying on the farm, well, maybe his father didn't know as much as he thought he did.

George spit on a corner of his shirtsleeve. He was just about to take out the trombone to shine it, when he froze. From the grey mist came the song of the first meadowlark. Bright gold etched in black, the bird boldly flew to a nearby fence post and sang and sang. When the meadowlark paused, George cupped his hands to his mouth and whistled perfectly, note for note, its sweet, wild music. The bird echoed. But this time it seemed to ask, "How-far-do-you-think-that-you-will-go?"

Without warning, a tightness gripped George's chest. It was the same kind of feeling he had had when he was young and it was night and the wolves were howling.

What if he never played before a real audience? What if he never did anything outstanding and exciting with his life? What if he never escaped Oak Hollow?

The meadowlark flapped its wings. Wistfully, George watched the bird disappear into the fog. "It's only a song," he told himself. But the haunting music echoed in his ears.

2 TRAVELING PHOTOGRAPHER

"Stranger's coming!" six-year-old Burt crowed triumphantly. He waved his arms from atop the soddy roof, which was spangled with the tiny blue-and-white grass flowers of early May. "Told you I'd spot the first wagon today."

George frowned. He scrambled up the ladder to join his brother and make certain he wasn't lying. Sure enough, in the distance he could see an unfamiliar, battered, green covered wagon with white lettering painted on it. The road from the town of Defiance, just five miles away, had been impassable for weeks because of spring rain. Undaunted, the horse pulling the wagon struggled through churned-up patches of mud thick and sticky enough to suck off a man's boots.

"Boys!" Mother called. "Who is it?"

"Says 'photographer' on the front," Burt replied, giving George a smug grin. Burt and Pa had the same thin-lipped, stubborn mouth.

"The photographer!" Mother exclaimed. "This is our chance to have a family picture taken."

"How we going to have a family picture without Addie?" Burt asked.

"It can't be helped that she's still away," Mother replied. "We may not have another opportunity like this in a long while. Climb down, Burt, and tell your father the traveling photographer's coming. Seeding will have to wait." Mother darted inside the soddy and began dragging chairs and nail kegs out to the yard. She placed them in a row.

George watched, fascinated. What would the photographer do when he arrived? Would chores be cancelled because of his unexpected visit?

"Lost the bet, George. I saw his wagon first," Burt said. He spoke quietly so that Mother, who forbade gambling, could not hear him. "Hand over the slingshot."

Reluctantly, George removed his favorite slingshot from the pocket of his overalls. It was made of peeled-smooth cottonwood and had a genuine India-rubber strap. Burt crossed his arms and fixed his brother with a merciless dark-eyed stare. "Give it to me," he demanded.

Was the slingshot worth a fight? George knew Pa would give him and Burt a thrashing if they wrestled on the roof. And George knew he'd get all the blame. How many times a day did his parents say, "George, set a good example. You're the oldest child in the family now. Act responsibly."

Fighting, George knew, was not acting responsibly. He sighed. Before Addie left, he had thought his new position in the family would give him power and glory. But he soon discovered that being the oldest was just another chore and bother. When he wasn't keeping an eye on headstrong, four-year-old Nellie May, he was protecting eight-year-old Lew from schoolyard bullies. The rest of the time he had to put up with Burt's wild dares. Who could slide headfirst in the snow down from the highest bluff to the Jim River? Who could walk out farthest on the frozen slough before the ice broke?

"Here, take the dumb slingshot," George grumbled. He wished he had never made the bet. As long as he could remember, Burt had never lost a bet or backed down from a dare. "Just don't shoot it at anybody."

Without hesitation, Burt picked up a clump of sod and aimed the slingshot at Lew, who sat reading on the ground below. PFFFFFFFZZZZZITTTT!

"Ouch!" Lew howled. He raised his blond, fuzzy head up from his book in time to catch Burt's angelic smile. "Mother, Burt is shooting dirt at me!"

"Burt, stop that!" Mother scolded. "I told you to climb down here and get Pa. Lew, herd the new mules to this end of the corral so they can be in the picture. George,

I need your help, too. You bring out the table."

George and Burt climbed reluctantly down from the roof using the ladder leaning against the house. "Tattletale," Burt hissed as he passed Lew. Lew looked away, as if he had not heard. But George could see that his cheeks were flushed with shame. Like his brothers, Lew knew that tattling to Mother was considered cowardly and downright girlish.

"Shut up, Burt. Leave him alone!" George snapped. He watched Lew nervously try to brush the mud from his pant leg. Lew had the thinnest, boniest wrists and ankles. His nose always ran. He couldn't play winter sports because cold weather made his lips turn blue and his teeth chatter. He'd rather stay inside where it was warm and read another book.

"Don't tell me what to do, Big Britches," Burt whispered to George. "Remember, I'm the one with the slingshot now."

George fumed as he went inside the house. When he returned with the table, he dragged it to the end of the row of chairs. Mother unfolded her fanciest linen cloth and spread it carefully so that the rough table legs did not show. She stood back to examine her work. "Bring out my geranium, Nellie May," she said. "And mind that you don't drop it."

The delicate geranium had survived four Dakota

winters planted indoors in an Arbuckle Coffee can. Whenever the temperature dropped, Mother carefully wrapped the flower in an old quilt and set it beside the potbelly stove, away from the worst icy drafts. Each spring it bloomed again, much to her joy.

Nellie thumped the coffee can on the table. Then she went back inside to get the box containing her snakeskin collection. She placed this on the rocking chair in the middle of the row. "This is my seat. I'm going to bring out my rag doll and my hobbyhorse, too."

"Nellie May, go inside quick and change your clothes. I put your new sateen dress on the bed, and your striped socks and good shoes, too," Mother said. "When you're dressed, I'll comb your hair into pretty ringlets."

"Ringlets make my eyes squinty," Nellie whined.

"That's fine, dear heart," Mother responded absent-mindedly. She opened the big family Bible and placed it on the table as Nellie May stomped inside.

It was very like his sister, George thought, to plan on sitting in the very center of the photograph. After all, Nellie May was the baby, the darling of the family, the only one who could do no wrong. It wasn't fair.

"George, don't just stand there," Mother said. "Go wash your face and put on your good shirt."

"Yes, ma'am," George replied sullenly. He hated his uncomfortable, starched shirt with the sleeves that crept up to his elbows. Maybe a visit from a photographer wasn't so wonderful after all.

"Pa!" Nellie called, bounding through the doorway in her new dress. "Swing me 'round! I want to see if my skirt twirls out like wings!"

Pa, who had just come from the field, stood at the pump. He took off his wide-rimmed hat, exposing his high, white forehead, the only part of his face that wasn't sunburned. After splashing water on his face, he ran his wet hands through his thinning brown hair and wiped himself dry with a flour sack. "Don't you know the photographer's coming?" He paused, hands on his hips, looking sternly down at his bossy little daughter. "We have to get ready, Nellie."

"Just one time 'round!" she begged.

Pa's twinkling blue eyes betrayed him. "All right. Just this once," he said. Nellie May had a way with Pa. She softened him. And he seemed to enjoy spoiling her. He took Nellie's hands and twirled her around so fast that her feet left the ground.

"Look at me, everybody! I'm flying!" she squealed happily.

A smile flashed across Mother's face; then she frowned. "This is no time to be silly, Samuel! Go put on your paper collar. The photographer will be here any moment. Do you think we should sprinkle some hay on the mud near the barn?" She pointed toward the huge frame structure. Built at considerable expense two years ago, the barn was the only one of its kind for miles. "I would hate for the folks back in Iowa to see our picture and think we keep a messy farm."

"I'm afraid there's no time, Becca," Pa said. "Here comes the photographer now."

The mud-caked wagon creaked into the yard. "Hello!" the driver called exuberantly. He was a tall, energetic man with a black moustache. When he jumped to the ground, his blue eyes danced. Dramatically, he swept off his derby hat, revealing dark, slicked-back hair. Most men simply tipped their hats in front of women. Mother smiled, pleased by this stranger's unusual, gallant gesture.

"The name's Harold Neidacorn, photographic artist. And you're Doc Mills, unless I'm mistaken," he said, shaking Pa's hand. "I've heard all about you and your wonderful homestead from folks way over in Charles Mix County. Glad I found you at home so I could offer you my services. 'Save the substance ere the shadow fades'— that's my motto."

"We'd be pleased to have our picture taken," Pa said, beaming with pride. The nickname "Doc" had been given to him by local homesteaders who trusted his know-how and common sense. Four years of successfully raising large, fine herds of cattle, horses, and mules had earned him the reputation of a respected stockman. Although he had no formal training as an animal doctor, he constantly read ranching manuals and medical digests to keep up-to-date on the latest cures for livestock diseases.

"How many head of cattle do you have?" Mr. Neidacorn asked as he unloaded equipment from his wagon.

"Three hundred head on about 320 acres. Just bought a whole herd of Kentucky Jack mules which I intend to breed and break. Muleskinners hauling cargo to the Black Hills tell me they're always looking for strong, intelligent lead animals."

"Sounds like you've got a real head for business. What do you plan to do with your profits?" Mr. Neidacorn carried a clumsy black box and set it on a wooden tripod. He opened the box and out popped an accordionlike contraption with a glass lens.

Pa smiled. "Buy more land, of course. Now if you'll excuse me, I'm going to change into a clean shirt. I'll be right back."

Mr. Neidacorn attached a black viewing cloth to the back of the camera and winked at George, who watched him in wonder. As soon as Pa returned, Mr. Neidacorn said, "I've been to the Black Hills. There's some fine country west of the Missouri for ranching, if the government ever breaks up the reservation."

Pa shook his head. "That west river country is too

far away and too dangerous. I'll build up my holdings right here in Hutchinson County." He took out his gold pocket watch that nobody could touch except him. Carefully, he flipped open the lid, checked the time, and put it back in his pocket. "I don't mean to rush you, Mr. Neidacorn, but I'm a bit behind schedule today and I've got quite a few chores to finish. See here, do you think you could get our new Reliance windmill into the photograph? Pumps down nearly sixty feet. George, bring Mr. Neidacorn a sample."

George filled a dipper of the cool well water for the photographer. Mr. Neidacorn thanked George and gulped noisily. "You're one of the lucky ones, Doc Mills," he said.

"Yes, sir. It certainly helps to have luck. But it also takes hard work to get ahead in the world," Pa replied. "Luck and hard work—that's what's made Oak Hollow the finest homestead in all of Hutchinson County."

George winced. Pa's words sounded so boastful.

"Now let's get down to business," Mr. Neidacorn said. "It will take me only a few minutes to prepare the glass plates with chemicals." He climbed into the wagon and fastened the flap behind himself.

"George," Pa said quietly as he patted Mr. Neidacorn's bony horse, "slip on a bag of oats for this animal. He looks as if he could use it. I guess there's not much of a living to be made traveling around taking people's pictures."

"Mr. Neidacorn seems happy enough," George mumbled.

"Happy don't pay the rent."

Again George winced. What if the photographer had overheard Pa's remark? Hurriedly, George went to the barn, filled a feed bag, and hung it around the horse's neck.

"Now, let's take our seats quickly, please," called Mr. Neidacorn, emerging from the wagon. Holding the edges, he carried a rectangular piece of glass smeared with something that smelled strong and foul. He set the glass inside the back of the camera. "You want the dog in the picture?"

"Sure, he's part of the family," said Burt. He tipped dangerously back in his chair and motioned to the family's big black mutt, Buffalo, who had wandered in from the field. Buffalo sat down by Burt and started scratching himself. Burt laughed.

"It's too bad you came before our eldest daughter returned from school," Mother said, taking a seat beside Nellie May. "She's in her first year of high school at Yankton."

"Ah, yes. I read about the famous Miss Mills in the *Dakota Citizen*," Mr. Neidacorn said. "You should be proud

23

to have such a fine student in the family."

Mother blushed with pride. George rolled his eyes. He did not want to hear again about how Addie had skipped a grade or how her test scores were better than those of every other student in the county—including every boy.

"Think how happy your scholar will be to have such a valuable remembrance. A portrait of her parents, brothers, and sister," Mr. Neidacorn said.

Mother smiled. She ran her nervous fingers around the neat bun at the nape of her neck. Although she was only thirty-one years old, her thick, dark hair was beginning to streak with silver. "Our next oldest is George," she said. "I suppose he should sit at the end. Then comes Lew. Burt you move over here beside Nellie May. Samuel, you can sit on the end next to me."

George glanced at his brothers and sister. Burt spit on his hand, flattened down his cowlick, and made sure the slingshot was prominently displayed in his front pocket. Lew clutched *Robinson Crusoe,* a favorite book given to him by Addie. Nellie May knotted one hand in the mane of her hobbyhorse. In her other she held a precious, faceless rag doll, whose features she had long ago kissed away. George felt as if he were the only one not displaying some special belonging.

"Pa," George said quietly, "do you think I could go

inside and get the trombone? It would look shiny and pretty, I bet, in the picture."

Mother's back straightened. Pa's eyes narrowed. Immediately, George wished he hadn't brought up the subject.

"The trombone does not belong to you, George," Pa said in an even voice. "It's only borrowed."

George gulped. What would Pa do when he found out the truth? "I know, but—"

"Are we just about ready?" Mr. Neidacorn interrupted, poking his head up from behind the camera.

"I just thought I could run inside and get it, seeing as how I play in the Defiance Brass Band and how everyone else..." George's voice drifted off miserably. His father glared.

Pa didn't understand about music. He had already given George his opinion on the subject of trombone playing. "It's a plain waste of time," Pa had said. "Nobody I know ever made a living sliding a trombone back and forth. It's impractical and it keeps you from chores and schoolwork."

"Mother?" George whispered imploringly.

Mother looked at Pa's stony expression and shook her head. It was obvious she did not want to begin a family argument right in front of Mr. Neidacorn. Mother was proud of George's musical ability; she had told him so many times. But she also warned him that she was afraid one day he'd play in a dance-hall band. Dancing was against her strict Methodist upbringing. "I'm afraid not, George," Mother replied quietly. She gave Mr. Neidacorn a forced smile.

By now the sun was shining in everyone's eyes. Buffalo stood up and walked away. Nellie May whined that her shoes squeezed her feet. Burt and Lew jabbed each other. Pa continued to frown.

"Isn't anyone going to smile?" Mr. Neidacorn said cheerfully.

"Smile!" Pa commanded.

"George, you're not smiling," Mr. Neidacorn said.

Angrily, Pa stood up from his chair, went to the side of the soddy, and grabbed a pitchfork. "If you have to have something to hold, hold this," Pa said. "Now smile like you're the one who'll own all this fine land one day."

George tried to smile. He tried to look like the oldest, the responsible son, the one who planned to do the right thing by following in his father's footsteps. But deep down, George knew he was only pretending. Deep down, George hated farming. The thing George loved best was playing the trombone. His stomach twisted as he contemplated a new, horrible thought. What if Pa made him return the beautiful instrument to Mr. Finch and ask for his money back?

"Well, now, that's a bit better," Mr. Neidacorn said. The camera made a loud click. "Let's try another, shall we? I think the little girl's eyes were closed." Mr. Neidacorn removed the glass and ducked into the wagon. In a few moments, he reappeared with a new piece of glass. He slipped this inside the camera and checked the focus. "Good, but you all look a bit stiff and worried. Relax. Try and be as natural as possible. There, that's better. I consider myself an artist at creating lifelike and revealing photographs. One of my best portraits is of Sylvester Rawding and his family over near Enemy Creek in Davison County. Maybe you know Mr. Rawding?"

Pa shook his head.

"He was here before your time, perhaps," Mr. Neidacorn continued. "Now, there was a man who seemed to have plenty of luck. He fought in the Civil War and had the good fortune to come away alive in an accident that would have killed most soldiers." Click. He hurried nimbly with the glass plate to the wagon and returned with another. "One last try. Where was I? Oh, yes. It seems Mr. Rawding fought near Mobile, Alabama, and was shot right over his left eye. Never removed the musketball, yet he wasn't blinded. You can see the hole in his forehead plain as day in my picture. Well, I'll tell you something, two years after I took that photograph, I went back to their homestead. Found out the son had duped the old man into deeding the ranch over to him. Evicted Sylvester Rawding and forced him into an old soldier's home in Kansas. How do you like that?" Click.

"Humph," Pa replied. "Sounds to me like bad blood."

"I'm not an expert," Mr. Neidacorn said, pulling out the last glass plate. "But I'll tell you what I've noticed. The frontier is hard on families. Harder than we like to believe sometimes. Out here on the prairie, a family is separated from some part of itself. Some part gone on farther west or some part left behind back East, maybe in Illinois or Michigan. Isolation and hardship, confusion and fear—they can make people do desperate things."

"Dakota is the best place on earth I know of," Pa said with great certainty.

Mr. Neidacorn threw back his head and laughed as he carried away the third plate of glass. "Soon as Dakota makes itself a state, you ought to run for the legislature, Doc. I mean that as a compliment."

Pa smiled. "How much do we owe you?"

"Three dollars," Mr. Neidacorn called from inside the wagon. "I'd appreciate cash, although people have been known to pay me in smoked hams, bags of feathers, or watermelons."

"Sure, I've got cash," Pa said. "You children run along now while I pay Mr. Neidacorn. Becca, maybe you can find him something to eat?"

Mother took Nellie May firmly in one hand and walked toward the soddy. "Don't try to run off and dirty that pretty new dress! Lew and Burt, you come inside, too, and change your clothes. George, will you bring out some food for Mr. Neidacorn?" Mother fixed a plate of salt pork, beans, and fresh bread slathered with butter and chokecherry preserves, and George carried the dinner out to the yard. He stood shyly beside Mr. Neidacorn and Pa as they loaded the wagon with the camera and supplies.

"Pleasure doing business with you," Pa said. He gave Mr. Neidacorn three silver dollars. They shook hands. "I've got to check on my cows—calving's started. You'll send word from Defiance when our pictures are ready?"

"In three days they'll be printed," Mr. Neidacorn promised. He took the plate from George and sat on the back of the wagon.

Pa waved farewell and started out to the field. "You coming, George?"

George nodded. "In just a minute." He knew he should follow his father, but instead he lingered. He couldn't help himself. Mr. Neidacorn was the first person he had ever met who called himself an artist.

"Sit yourself down," Mr. Neidacorn said, motioning to George. George took a seat beside him and cleared his throat. He did not know what to say. Mr. Neidacorn took a bite of beans and said in a friendly, natural way,

"Well, that was a fair easy piece. I've taken pictures of every kind of soldier and sodbuster between here and the Niobrara River. I can tell you all sessions don't go so smoothly."

"They don't?" George asked. Was Mr. Neidacorn only politely pretending he had not noticed the humiliating argument over the trombone?

"I remember one time a woman made me and her husband drag their brand-new pump organ clear across the yard so the family could set up a pose as far away from the house as she could get. Seems she didn't want the photograph to be taken anywhere near their dugout."

"Why?"

"She didn't want her family back in Connecticut to know she lived in a house shoveled out of the side of a hill. I'd say that picture was one of the hardest of the two thousand images I've taken in the past seven years."

"How did you learn how to do this business—art, I mean?" George hoped he didn't sound rude.

Mr. Neidacorn grinned and rubbed his chin. "Taught myself. You see, I started out as a carpenter. Something practical. But I never really liked the work. So I saved my money and bought a camera. I read everything I could. Soon as I had my chance, I left Valentine, Nebraska, and went on the road. I've traveled with the cavalry, the U.S. mail, and a couple of treaty commissions. Produced a fine set of stereoscopic pictures of landscapes and Indian views—chiefs, warriors, and children so lifelike you'd swear they were standing right in front of you. Ever look through a stereoscope?"

George shook his head.

Mr. Neidacorn reached into the wagon and produced a mysterious box. Inside was a stereoscope exactly like the one George had admired in the Montgomery Ward catalog. Mr. Neidacorn slipped a long card into place. He held the wooden handle so that George could look through the viewer, which was shaped like blinders on a horse.

George gasped. Before him was a new and strange landscape with colored buttes rising in fantastic shapes. In the distance rode a proud warrior on horseback. Everything looked so real! George felt as if he could almost reach out and touch the rocks and hear the horse whinny.

"That's the Badlands. Quite a place, when you see it in three dimensions, isn't it?" Mr. Neidacorn said. "I do all the color tinting myself. The brave's name is Blunt Arrow. One of the best horsemen I've ever seen."

George could hardly bear to stop looking. The Badlands was part of the great, mysterious, faraway world that he had only dreamed about. How he wished he could be as wild and free as Blunt Arrow and never have to plant corn or rake hay or herd mules again!

"There's nothing like travel," Mr. Neidacorn said, repacking his stereoscope. "Most people seldom go anyplace. My stereoscopic views let them escape from their everyday lives. I'm hoping to sell these views out East as soon as I find a buyer for my studio. I need to raise some money for my next big venture."

"You're leaving?"

Mr. Neidacorn laughed. "Once I get enough cash together, I'm heading for California. Plenty to photograph there—all kinds of exotic people and places."

George did not say anything. He watched Mr. Neidacorn hungrily sop up gravy with his bread. With a shabby handkerchief, he dabbed his moustache. The tips of his fingers were discolored by chemicals. Would he ever be able to wash away the dark stains?

"Some people call me a fool," Mr. Neidacorn said. "Others call me a crank. But I am much too interested in my work to pay any attention to such people. Life is an adventure. Seize the light. Follow your vision, that's what I say."

George was stunned. How did Mr. Neidacorn know that he secretly longed for adventure far from home? Could Mr. Neidacorn read his mind? Nervously, George cracked his knuckles. Pa would certainly call such advice impractical, foolish, and dangerous. George could just imagine his father's reply: "What has following some vision

33

ever done for Mr. Neidacorn? His suit's ragged. His horse is starving. He has no land, no house, no family. The man's crazy."

Without thinking, George jumped down from the wagon. "Whoa, there, George," Mr. Neidacorn said. "Before you go, would you mind returning this plate to your kind mother? Please thank her for the delicious repast."

"Yes, sir," George said.

Mr. Neidacorn smiled and reharnessed the horse. Then he climbed atop the wagon seat. "Don't look so frightened, George," he said, shaking the reins. "Follow your dream. See where the journey takes you." The wagon creaked out of the yard. Mr. Neidacorn turned, merrily waved his hat, and gave George a startling wink.

George waved weakly. Although he could hear his father calling to him, for some reason he could not move. He felt bewitched. He watched Mr. Neidacorn's rattletrap wagon until it vanished. Instead of being relieved that the man and his disturbing ideas were gone, George felt only a hollow sadness. Slowly, he walked back to the soddy, returned the plate, and dutifully joined his father in the field.

3 UGLY COW

May 15, 1887

Dear George,

Got the photograph today. I have been looking at it every chance I can—I am so homesick! I miss everyone. Mother looks very lovely, don't you think? And Pa seems so handsome and proud. Mother sent me a piece of the plaid sateen she used to make Nellie's dress, which came out very well. Burt and Lew look much older. But the one I hardly recognize is you, George. You look so angry. Maybe it's just because the sunlight is shining in your eyes.

Please write and tell me every detail of home. How many calves does Pa have now? I look at the photograph and pretend I can peer right inside the soddy door and see Mother's rocking chair and smell bread baking in the oven. Don't laugh at me, it's true. I have had no appetite for a week, and Mrs. Carlson worries I will perish. I am so anxious to be home again! Please don't tell Mother or Pa or they will worry.

George, you shouldn't tease so much about surprises!

I'm glad to hear you are practicing your trombone. Maybe you will give me a concert when I get home. Don't get behind in your studies just because school is out during the epidemic. I hope no one in the family gets the measles. Especially Lew. He isn't as strong as the rest of you.

You might think I never have any fun, but I do. Before the thaw, some girls from school and I went ice skating regularly on the pond in the middle of town. We have not tried rollerskating because it costs twenty-five cents.

It is nearly midnight and I must finish my studies. We have one more geography and civil government test in the morning. I hope I get good grades.

Love,

Addie

P.S. Please don't show this letter to anyone.

That evening, as soon as George finished reading his sister's letter, he hid it with the others in a creamed-corn can he kept in the barn loft. Addie wrote two kinds of letters—sickeningly cheerful letters for Mother and Pa, and refreshingly honest letters to him. She trusted George to keep her letters private. It amazed him how much better he liked his sister ever since she had left for school. She seemed to get along better with him, too. Was it because of their letters, he wondered? Sharing thoughts and dreams on paper was so much easier than trying to talk about them.

George understood almost everything that Addie told him in her letters. Everything except her homesickness. What was so wonderful about Oak Hollow? George would trade places with his sister in a minute for a chance to get away. How lucky she was to ice skate with friends and stay up until midnight whenever she wished!

George came inside and got ready for bed. "Blow out that candle and go to sleep, George," Mother called through the doorway of the lean-to, where George slept with Burt and Lew. His brothers were already asleep.

George did not want to go to sleep. He wanted to stay up until midnight, just like Addie. But try as he might, he soon drifted off.

It was still dark as pitch when he heard Pa's voice. "Get dressed, George," Pa whispered. "I need help with Ugly Cow. It's her time."

George staggered around Burt's bed and pulled on his overalls over his nightshirt. He stumbled past Buffalo and felt the damp ground with his bare foot to find his boots. Then he headed outside. Even in the dark he knew his way around the barnyard. This was probably his six-thousandth trip between the soddy and the barn, he thought sleepily.

When he wasn't doing regular chores, such as milking the cows or feeding the pigs, he was helping Pa with plowing and planting. Now it was calving season, which meant that George also had to make sure the new calves were eating properly and that they weren't showing any signs of sickness. And three or four times a day, he and Pa went out to the far pasture to bring in newborn calves before prowling coyotes found them. They herded the cows and their new babies into the fenced pasture closest to the barn.

Ordinarily, a cow calved by herself. She simply lay quietly, chewing her cud, and got up to look behind herself every now and then. As soon as the calf was born, the cow efficiently ate the afterbirth, licked her baby clean, fed it, and then rested.

Sometimes the cows and calves needed help. Mother used to assist Pa with calving; now that George was old enough, Pa had made him his regular assistant. At first, George was pleased that Pa picked him. But after being awakened from a deep sleep every night for the past week, George dreaded the job.

"Over here," Pa called to George. He was standing beside the last stall. A lantern hung overhead. Pa was scowling—a bad sign, George knew. His father seemed to sense instinctively which cows were going to have problems; he moved these animals into the barn, where he could keep watch on them.

"How is she?" George asked. Ugly Cow's sides heaved. She looked around at George with enormous, pain-filled eyes. Ugly Cow had never had so much trouble before. But she wasn't a young cow and this wasn't her first calf.

"It's coming backwards," Pa said. Instead of being born the normal way, snout and forelegs first, the calf was coming hind legs first. Ugly Cow sank into the hay. "You're going to have to tail her."

George cracked his knuckles. He rubbed his eyes to try and wake himself. He did not want Pa to be angry at him for making mistakes. What if they lost Ugly Cow? She had cost thirty-five dollars and was one of their best milkers.

As soon as Ugly Cow struggled to get on her feet, George grabbed the heavy, cumbersome tail and pulled backwards to give her the leverage she needed to stand. George admired the way Pa expertly tied a lariat around the cow's neck, then twice around a nearby post. Pa seemed to know nearly everything there was to know about animals. He could pick out one black calf from sixty others in a herd and tell exactly which cow the calf had come from, which bull had sired him, and who his grandparents were. Hadn't he set Buffalo's broken leg just right when the dog got caught under a wagon wheel? Everyone else said the poor pup would have to be shot. But not Pa.

"Hold the end of the rope and brace yourself if she throws her head," Pa commanded. "If she starts to choke, turn her loose."

George nodded. Pa never asked for George's opinion or said, "Why don't you maybe try this?" He would just tell George or his brothers exactly what he wanted done, and they'd better do it right the first time. That was the way Pa was.

Pa rolled up his sleeves and dunked his arm in a pail of sudsy water. Carefully, he slipped his arm all the way to the elbow inside Ugly Cow, trying to locate the calf's feet. Ugly Cow pushed against Pa. He tugged at the calf. Now George could see the unborn calf's waxy, yellowish back hooves pointing toward the barn roof instead of toward the floor, the way they were supposed to.

Pa fastened a rope to the calf's feet and tied it tight. He flexed his knees, leaned back, and pulled as hard as he could. Nothing happened. Pa was not a big man, but he was strong. He put his foot against the cow and gave a tug. Ugly Cow bellowed.

Ordinarily, a cow does not cry in pain. George shuddered and for a moment loosened his grip on the lariat. He felt as if he might throw up. But what would Pa say? George tried to ignore his squeamish stomach and instead concentrate on pulling the lariat tight.

The cow sank again. "Tail her!" Pa ordered. George pulled up on the tail. His back ached from holding the tail in one hand and the lariat with the other. Slowly, slowly, the calf's wet, matted slender legs emerged. George felt hopeful, even though he knew that Ugly Cow had no strength left. If only she would not give up!

Pa, his shirt dark with sweat, tried again and again to turn the calf. But he could not get a good grip; his arms were too big, and the calf was too slippery. Nothing seemed to work. "Pity to lose the calf. Must weigh close to sixty pounds," he muttered, out of breath. "But I'm more worried about losing the mother."

George and Pa struggled for what seemed like hours. They took turns tugging, and little by little, the calf emerged. Every so often Pa would check to make sure it was still alive. If worst came to worst, he'd have to cut up the dead calf and take it out in pieces. George tried not to think about that.

Finally, just as the sun began to shine through cracks in the east barn wall, Pa and George pulled together, and the head and shoulders surged out. The calf flopped into the hay, where it lay coated with the gleaming transparent birth sac that had been its protection. Its eyes had a terrified, faraway look. Pa swiftly hoisted the slippery animal in his arms and swung it back and forth, upside down, to drain the fluid from its lungs so it could breathe. Then he laid the calf on the ground and knelt beside it, pumping its chest. "Rub it with this rag to get its circulation going," Pa told George.

George worked furiously to save the animal. Suddenly the calf gasped, shook its head, and slung snot all over George. George reared back and yelled triumphantly, "He's all right!"

The calf kicked. George looked at Pa to see if he was smiling. He wasn't. "Wrong kind of kick," Pa said in a tired, matter-of-fact voice.

George wiped the snot from his face with his shirt. Desperately, he tried to boost the calf to its feet, but it would not budge. Ugly Cow's baby was dead.

"Help me, George," Pa said. Ugly Cow was sinking down on her knees. All the life seemed to have gone out of her.

"She going to be all right?" George whispered. He was trembling. He had seen animals born before. He had seen them die. But somehow he couldn't get used to it.

"Get me some fresh water," Pa said.

George ran to the pump. But as he bent over to fill the bucket, he noticed the blood and slime covering the front of his overalls. The next thing he knew, he was doubled over, throwing up.

"Where's that bucket?" Pa hollered from the barn.

George picked up the bucket and stumbled to the stall. But the minute he arrived, he knew it was too late. He could tell by the grim look on his father's face. "What took you so long?" Pa demanded.

George lowered the bucket to the ground. "She's dead, too?"

His father's mouth tightened and his back straightened. "You have to expect death when you raise livestock. That's part of the business," he said gruffly. "Now go on and clean yourself up. Try and get some sleep."

Why couldn't Pa show his disappointment like any other human being? Why did he always have to control his feelings, no matter what? George took a step forward. "Pa?" he called softly.

"What is it now?"

George wanted to ask if they had done everything they could. He wanted to hear Pa say that, yes, when he had been twelve years old, he felt just as shaken, just as queasy.

"Speak up, will you?" Pa asked impatiently.

"Nothing," George mumbled. He beat a hasty retreat to the pump. What good would talking do? After all, Pa never admitted that he was uncertain.

George splashed freezing water on his arms, his neck, his face. Try as he might, he could not shake from his mind the way Ugly Cow had looked at him, her eyes filled with so much suffering, so much pain. Vigorously, he rubbed a chunk of lye soap between his hands, even though he knew the suds would not wash away the smell of cow. There was no way to get rid of that smell until calving season ended. Then some new season would begin—the season the sows farrowed or the season the steers had to be branded—and some new smell would linger on his hands, on his clothes, in his hair.

The bitter fact was that, unlike Pa, he felt no sense of accomplishment from farm work. That was the difference between farming and music. When George played a piece on his trombone, there was a beginning, a middle, and an end. He had created something—a melody. But when he worked on the farm, he just seemed to do the same hard, dirty, dull chores over and over again. Nothing was ever really finished. And what was the point?

George pulled off his mud- and straw-caked boots and flung them angrily outside the soddy door. He would never follow in his father's footsteps. Never.

4 WHAT MR. NEIDACORN SAID

The next day the weather seemed warm as summer. George's best friend, Shiloh Fairchild, stood outside the Mills' soddy and dug his big, dirty toe into the mud. Good old Shy! A little Dakota gumbo never bothered him. He wore his brown cap with the broken visor pulled down to keep the sun out of his pale blue eyes. Slung over one shoulder were man-sized shoes with their broken laces tied together. George had never known Shy to wear shoes when he didn't have to. "Can't think all laced up," Shy always said, a slow smile spreading across his broad, freckled face.

George, who stood at the window, waved to his friend. Shy waved back. Beside him was the Fairchild's bony horse. Lashed across the saddle was a rusty plow.

Burt flung open the door and snapped his slingshot so that the older boy would be sure to notice it. "Hello, Shy!" he called respectfully. No one at Hutchinson County's school could outshoot, outjump, or outwrestle Burt's hero.

"Hello yourself!" hollered husky, dark-haired Shy. "Is George ready? He told me I should get here bright and early to go to town. Something about groceries for your ma. Pa told me I have to get his plow sharpened at the blacksmith's."

"Mother's finishing her list right now," Burt said. He snapped the slingshot again.

"Say, isn't that George's?" Shy asked. From his pocket he pulled his all-purpose pocketknife with the black horn handle. Shy used this knife to trim his fingernails, eat his lunch, skin gophers, or carve his name in the school outhouse door. Now he expertly whittled the end of a stick, then used it to clean between his large front teeth.

"The slingshot *was* George's. Now it's mine," Burt replied, loud enough for George to hear.

George stood at the kitchen table, impatiently waiting for Mother to finish counting the grocery money. He felt surprised that his brother's boast did not make him mad. Maybe the slingshot didn't mean that much to him anymore. Or maybe he had too many other things on his mind.

"Now don't forget the four good-sized lemons and the pound of raisins," Mother said. She handed George a slip of brown paper.

"Does Pa know about the lemons?" George asked, looking at Mother's neatly written list. Pa always kept careful records of every expenditure Mother made. It irritated George the way Pa always saw fit to remind everyone that "a penny saved is a penny earned." Now that the farm was finally doing well, why couldn't the family enjoy an extravagance once in a while without having to hear the same old aggravating warning?

"Pa knows about the lemons," Mother said, and sighed. "I need fresh lemons and raisins to make lemon raisin pie. It's Addie's favorite. I want it to be a special surprise when she comes home tomorrow."

"Oh," George said in a small voice. Didn't Mother remember that lemon raisin pie was his favorite, too?

"You look tired, George. You were up late last night with that poor cow and her calf, weren't you?" Mother asked.

George nodded and turned away. He did not want to think about last night.

Mother put her hand on George's shoulder. "You're so quiet these days, George, ever since we had the photograph taken. Is something bothering you? Was it because of what Pa said about that trombone? You haven't seemed yourself. What's wrong?"

George shrugged her hand away. "I'm perfectly fine," he said sullenly.

"I know that what happened with Ugly Cow was very sad," Mother persisted. "But sometimes the cows and their calves just don't survive, in spite of everything we try. That's just the way life is."

George wanted Mother to stop talking, especially since Burt and Lew were eavesdropping. It was impossible to have a private conversation in the crowded soddy. Didn't Mother know that? Any show of weakness, any display of girlish squeamishness could be used against George by his brothers. Hadn't he done the same to them?

"I'm all right, Mother. Shy is waiting for me," George mumbled. He edged toward the door.

"Pa has had a lot on his mind lately," Mother said, her voice soft, almost pleading.

George lowered his glance. He did not want his mother to see his burning face. "I have to go now," he said.

"One last thing, George."

"What?"

"I want you to take Nellie May with you."

"Nellie May?" His trip to town was ruined!

"I have a lot of spring cleaning to finish today, and I'd like you to keep your eye on her so she stays out of mischief."

George groaned. "Do I have to? I don't see how I can manage. Shy has the plow to be sharpened and I have to haul all those groceries and—"

"I'm sure you can manage," Mother replied. "If she gets tired, you can easily carry her on your back. Now get along and don't linger in town longer than you have to. Nellie's out in the barn. Call to her and tell her she's to go with you. And make sure she takes a clean handkerchief. I'm afraid she's coming down with a bit of a cold."

"Yes, ma'am," George said miserably. A clean handkerchief! A pesky sister who would have to ride part way on his back was bad enough. But a pesky sister with a hideous, runny nose was even worse. George decided he had no luck at all. Absolutely none. He thrust the grocery list in his pocket, stomped past Lew, and joined Shy in the yard. Buffalo was happily circling the visitor, sniffing the scent of the Fairchilds' bloodhounds.

"What's riling you?" Shy asked. He gave Buffalo a playful rub on the head. "You look like you just swallowed a whole plug of tobacco."

"Bad news. We have to take Nellie May with us to town."

Shy moaned. "Oh, shoot! And I came all the way here thinking I'd left bossy women at home!"

"Sorry," George said. He motioned to Shy to follow him to the barn. George cupped his hands to his mouth and yelled, "Nellie! Where are you?"

"What do you want?" Nellie May demanded. She sneezed and peered over the edge of the barn loft, her skinny legs dangling.

"You're supposed to come to town with us," George said irritably. "And you better not be up there torturing those poor new kittens."

"Am not. I'm just dressing them up. They each have a little hat on and they don't mind it one bit. Can I really go with you, George? Did Mother say so?"

"Yes," George said. He rolled his eyes at Shy to indicate his disgust with all the females who ever lived.

"Yipeee!" Nellie May shouted. She scooted down the ladder at breakneck speed, her hair filled with hay wisps. "You can buy me a candy stick, all right, George? I want a red cinnamon kind. Not that yellow flavor that tastes like puke."

"It's not puke. It's pineapple. And I'm not wasting my money on you, so don't beg me for something you aren't going to get."

Nellie May took George's hand and skipped. Buffalo trotted at her heels. "You know I like you best, George. You're my favorite brother."

Shy shifted the horse's reins to his other hand. "I think she's up to something," he warned. "I know this trick. My sisters do this to me all the time."

"Who asked you?" Nellie May said, glaring.

"Nobody, Willy Nilly Nellie," Shy replied and grinned.

"Don't call me that awful name. That's not nice. So don't ever use it again."

"You talk so much you give me a headache, Nellie May," George complained.

Nellie dropped George's hand and began to pout.

"Why don't you look for buffalo bones?" George suggested, hoping to get rid of his sister so that he could talk to Shy alone.

"What will you give me if I do?" she asked. "How about a penny candy stick?"

George sighed.

Shy laughed. He stopped the horse, picked up a rock, and threw it for Buffalo to retrieve. "Now she's got you. See what I mean?"

"Nellie, can't you leave us in peace for one minute?" George shouted angrily. "Go look for bones and don't get lost. And don't step on any rattlers."

"You're the one who's scared of snakes. Not me," Nellie said. She stuck out her tongue and skipped over the next rise.

George's face flushed with anger and embarrassment.

Shy spit on the ground. "Sisters!" he said with contempt. "I got four I wish would leave me in peace, even for one second!"

George wiped sweat from his forehead, thankful Nellie was gone. "Say, Shy, you ever thought of leaving Dakota?" He put a stem of dry grass in his mouth and gave his friend a hopeful glance.

Shy looked surprised. "Nope, never have." Buffalo galloped into view. Shy took the rock from the dog's mouth and threw it again.

"Ever thought of going west to the Badlands or maybe to the Black Hills and visiting a big city like Deadwood—maybe prospecting for gold?"

"Shoot, why do you want to go to some forsaken place like the Badlands? And don't you know you can't get to the Black Hills from here without going north to Chamberlain? Then you got to cross the Missouri River. After that, you have to travel on the wagon road across the Sioux Indian reservation. Them Indians are all relatives of Sitting Bull, and they'd just as soon take your scalp as give you a how-de-do. Pa says nobody ought to use that road until the government finally breaks up the reservation once and for all."

"Well," George continued impatiently, "what about going to San Francisco? Ever think of going there?"

Shy scratched his head. "Nope, I suspect I never will. I don't want to."

"Why?"

"I like it here."

"I mean, when you grow up. Ever think of moving somewhere else?"

Shy chuckled. "Why should I? Pa says when he gets old he's going to give me the homestead. That's what

I'm going to do. I'm going to farm."

"What do you like so much about farming?" George demanded.

Shy did not answer right away. He took out his knife and hacked a piece of grass to ribbons, the way he always did when he was deep in thought. "When I'm outside doing field work, I watch things grow. I like the quiet. Gives me a chance to think."

"What do you think about?"

"Nothing."

"Do you believe life is an adventure?"

This question seemed to puzzle Shy. He hacked four more pieces of grass before he finally spoke. "Life is getting up in the morning, eating breakfast, doing chores, going to school, eating, going to school again, coming home, doing chores, eating again, and going to sleep. That's about it. I don't think there's anything real adventuresome about life until you grow up and you can stop going to school and do what you want."

"Well, what do you want to do when you grow up?"

"I already told you. I'm going to farm."

"You mean you never want to go anywhere else, do anything exciting?"

"What's the matter with you, George? You don't have to get so hopping mad. All right, maybe next year I'll go to the county fair and show my twin heifers and win first prize. Maybe the last day of class I'll set off firecrackers underneath the schoolhouse. Maybe on the Fourth of July I'll get to march in the Defiance Brass Band down Main Street, beating that big bass drum louder than anything. There, does that satisfy you?"

George sighed.

"George, you don't hardly seem like your old self. Maybe you need a dose of Dr. Guyott's Yellow Dock and Sarsaparilla. That's what Pa gives me when I get ornery from spring fever."

"I don't have spring fever," George growled. Buffalo returned with the rock and dropped it at the boys' feet. This time George picked it up and hurled it as hard as he could.

"Maybe you're coming down with the measles or something. Lots of people in town still have the spots. You remember that little girl you said your sister sat next to at church? Why, I heard—"

"I'm not sick," George interrupted. "I don't have the measles. I'm perfectly all right!" He spat out the piece of grass. For nearly a quarter of a mile, the boys walked along without speaking.

"Sorry, Shy," George said finally. "Didn't mean to blow up at you like that."

"It's all right, George. I know what your problem is. You think too much." Shy smiled and gave George a friendly shove, as was their custom.

George half-heartedly returned the shove. If Mr. Neidacorn had never told him that life was an adventure and that a person should follow his vision, maybe he wouldn't be feeling so unhappy about everything. Well, he'd just forget about what Mr. Neidacorn had said. It was obviously nonsense. Nothing more.

5 BARRETT TRAVELING THEATRE

"What's that?" Nellie May called to the boys. They had been walking for nearly an hour, with George sometimes carrying his sister. Now she was excitedly pointing to something on the next rise. Buffalo bounded ahead. As soon as George and Shy joined her, they could see it, too. Outside town, billowing like a breathing, sleeping dragon, was an enormous yellow tent. It flashed in the sunlight. "Think it's the circus?" Nellie asked hopefully.

"Maybe it's the one with the Russian rollerskaters and the ostreech and the sea lions and the grizzly bears!" Shy said.

"I read in the paper the circus doesn't come till next month," George replied. "Might be a revival meeting."

Nellie and Buffalo ran toward the tent.

"I hope it's not a revival meeting," George confided. "Mother will make me go for sure. I hate revival meetings.

Everybody talks and yells and thumps and sings and bores me silly. Worse yet, preachers come over for dinner and we can't act hardly human."

Shy wrinkled up his nose and nodded in agreement. For as long as George had known his friend, Shy had never gone to church. The only church in Hutchinson County gave a combination Episcopal-Methodist-Baptist service. But it wasn't the unusual liturgy that bothered Shy's pa. It was the waste of good daylight. "Whenever my pa has the chance, he likes to take the dogs and go hunting," Shy once explained. "Sunday is as good as any day to wander off and bag a dozen prairie chickens or a brace of wild ducks."

Shy's pa was born and raised in Kentucky. When his wife died, he moved his four daughters and Shy to Dakota, along with six purebred bloodhounds. The hounds howled and scampered in Shy's dugout and regularly gave the whole family fleas. But what were a few flea bites? The dogs were treated like royalty. They were the only fine things the Fairchild family owned.

Suddenly, a trumpet fanfare blasted from the tent.

"Shoot, ain't no band ever plays at a prayer meeting!" Shy shouted. "Let's take a look!" He gave his horse a whack on the rump, and it broke into a trot.

George read aloud the large sign that was outside the tent:

Barrett Traveling Theatre
See *King Lear* tonight!

We have toured the world and entertained royalty!

Featuring the famous star, Blanche De Mar,
the handsomest woman in the world!
See spectacular musicians perform!
Thrill to exciting stage numbers!

Murder! Love! Revenge!

Matinees on Wednesday, Thursday, Friday.

Shy tied the horse to a stake. He parted the tent flaps. "Come on!" George hissed, motioning to his sister.

"No," Nellie said. She flounced onto the ground, gripping Buffalo under her arm. "Me and Buffalo don't budge till you buy candy like you promised."

"Suit yourself," George muttered. "We'll be back in a few minutes. Don't wander off."

The boys hurried inside in time to see a horn player march off a low wooden stage at the far end of the tent. No one seemed to notice when the boys sat on one of the many benches. George took a deep breath. He liked the smell of the fresh sawdust that had been sprinkled on the ground.

On stage, a man with flowing white hair, a grey beard, and a long brown robe appeared like a specter in a dream. Light streamed through a rip in the tent roof, illuminating his anguished expression. He raised his arms and roared:

> *Blow, winds, and crack your cheeks!*
>> *rage! blow!*
> *You cataracts and hurricanes, spout*
> *Till you have drench'd our steeples,*
>> *drown'd the cocks!*

George felt the cold spray of a storm against his face. Not once did his gaze swerve from the ancient man. His musical language was baffling, bewitching. George had never before heard such beautiful words or seen such tragic poses. He forgot about Pa's argument over the trombone. He forgot about Ugly Cow. He forgot about everything. Instead, he felt as if he, too, were living in a faraway, stormy land filled with adventure.

When the scene ended, George jumped up and clapped and cheered loudly. He dragged Shy to his feet.

King Lear bowed. "Thank you, thank you!" he said. The old king leapt off the stage with surprising agility. "Did you enjoy the rehearsal?"

George could only nod as King Lear peeled off his grey beard and rubbed away his wrinkles with a towel. He removed his fine, white hair. In only a matter of moments, he was transformed into a handsome man with brown, curly hair, an unlined face, and a merry smile. Fantastic! How convenient, George thought, to be able to grow old or young, however it suited a person.

"Shoot, how'd you do that?" Shy asked, staring.

"Ah, that's *our* secret," a loud voice interrupted. Without warning, a tall, slender boy, not much older than George or Shy, swooped off the stage and landed gracefully nearby. He laughed and held out his hand. "My name is Jacob," he said, his black eyes dancing. "And this is Victor Barrett, owner and proprietor of the greatest traveling theatrical troupe west of the Mississippi."

Victor made another low bow. George and Shy were too stunned to speak. They had never met a famous person before.

"And who are you fine fellows?" Victor asked.

George and Shy introduced themselves, then shook hands with Victor. "How long will you be performing here, sir?" George asked shyly.

"As long as there's an audience," Victor said.

Jacob gave each boy a friendly clap on the back. "Tell your friends, your family."

Victor grinned. "Jacob's my regular right-hand man. I don't know what I'd do without him."

Jacob looked pleased. "Tickets are one dollar and fifty cents."

Shy gasped. "Shoot, that's a lot of money!"

George jabbed Shy to silence him before he said anything else embarrassing.

"For art, one dollar and fifty cents is a small price to pay," Jacob replied. "Where else in this godforsaken prairie can you see Shakespeare performed by professionals? Where else can you listen to skilled musicians who have played before royalty around the world?"

"Musicians? Around the world?" George asked in awe.

"That's right," Victor said, beaming with pride.

"Do they wear real...real band uniforms?"

Victor laughed. "Of course. Velvet jackets with gold braid."

"Do you have a trombone player?" George held his breath in anticipation.

"Amazing you should ask!" Jacob said.

Dolefully, Victor shook his head. "Unfortunately, during our engagement in Yankton, our trombonist's mother dragged her home. It was an ugly incident. The unenlightened woman seemed to think that the theatre was not a respectable profession for a young lady artist."

George could not imagine anything more respectable, more artistic than Victor Barrett or his theatre. What a life! Traveling around the world, visiting exciting cities, performing before thousands of people—not to mention kings and queens! It sounded glorious.

"Horace and Steele!" Victor called to two young men lounging on benches. "That castle nearly fell on me twice during rehearsal. I want you to fix it. *Now.*"

The tall, thin man stood up slowly. His bristly moustache matched his bristly eyebrows. "Steele here says it's unlucky to have a smooth dress rehearsal," he complained.

Steele nodded. He was short and dark with wavy black hair and a gaping expression that reminded George of a bullhead. "Smooth dress rehearsal means opening night disaster."

"Angels and ministers of grace defend us!" Victor said in his marvelous, booming voice.

Grumbling, Horace and Steele shuffled backstage. Jacob handed George a yellow theatre leaflet. "You may keep this," Jacob said. "I hope you'll come to our show some evening."

"Please, Mr. Barrett...would you sign it for me?" George stammered.

"Certainly! My King Lear rivals the best in any American theatre today." When Victor finished scribbling his autograph, he asked George, "Do I sound like I'm just bragging?"

"Absolutely not!" George blurted. "The way I figure, if you tell it true, it isn't bragging."

Jacob smiled. " 'If you tell it true, it isn't bragging.' I like that."

"It does have an honest ring to it," Victor agreed.

"Would it be all right if I used your phrase in some of our publicity materials?" Jacob asked.

62

George nodded, spellbound. Imagine! The Barrett Theatre using one of *his* phrases. "Jacob, would…would you mind signing, too?" he asked. Jacob made his signature neatly beside Victor's. George admired the dramatic handwriting:

Victor Barrett   Jacob Barrett

"Are you relatives by any chance?" George asked.

"Father and son, to be exact," Victor replied proudly.

Amazing! George never would have guessed that two people who called each other by their first names and treated each other as equals could ever possibly be father and son.

Even Shy, whose pa never ordered him around like a hired hand, seemed impressed. "Shoot," he said under his breath.

George sighed. He had only two dollars left since he bought the trombone. But he would gladly spend every last penny for a chance to visit Victor and Jacob Barrett and their marvelous theatre again. "Good luck on your first night!" he called.

To his surprise, Victor and Jacob looked horrified. "Say, 'break a leg.' Will you?" Jacob whispered.

"Break a leg?" George asked, confused. Why would he want to say such an awful thing?

"Just say it," Jacob insisted.

"Break a leg," George said.

Victor and Jacob smiled, waved, and disappeared behind the stage.

George and Shy stumbled outside into the bright light. "What was all that about busting legs?" Shy asked.

"Maybe it's a secret code. I wish I knew," George said wistfully. "Say, where did Nellie May wander off to? I thought she came in behind us."

"Last time I saw her she was over there," said Shy, pointing.

Scurrying around the tent, the boys found the horse still tied to a stake. Nellie May was nowhere in sight. "Nellie May!" George shouted. "Where are you?"

The boys hurried down the road toward town. A freighter was coming toward them, and they hailed it. The man perched on the seat of the loaded wagon whistled a signal, and the four teams of mules came to a halt. "You seen a big black dog and a little barefoot girl with brown hair?" George called to him.

The driver, an enormous bullwhacker with hairy arms, spit an impressive stream of tobacco juice. "Over yonder by the dry goods store."

"Thanks!" George called.

Sprawled on the boardwalk on the shady side of the store was Buffalo. Nearby sat Nellie May, arm-in-arm with a pale girl a year or two older who wore a raggedy print dress. The girl and Nellie May seemed to have become fast friends. Whenever the girl took a lick of the candy stick, she passed it to Nellie May. In turn, Buffalo cleaned Nellie's hands with his enormous tongue. Shy burst into laughter when he saw them.

"What are you doing?" George demanded. "Nellie May, why did you run off like that and scare me to death?" He wrenched the candy out of Nellie's hand and gave it back to the raggedy girl.

"Ella is my new best friend. She was just giving me a taste," Nellie May complained.

George disgustedly wiped his sticky hand on the back of his pants. He took a good look at Ella. Her grey eyes were red-rimmed, as though she were ready to burst into tears at any moment. Her hair was black and matted, and her sorrowful, thin face was covered with red spots. "Say, what's that all over your face?" he asked.

"Nothing," Ella mumbled. She lifted her apron over her head and ran away.

"Nellie May, didn't you see what was on her face?" George demanded.

"No," Nellie said indignantly. "It's rude to make fun of people that have flea bites. That's what you say, George. See how you hurt Ella's feelings? You're nasty."

George grumbled, "I only hope those spots weren't

something worse."

"Her candy tasted all right. Least she was willing to share." Nellie sniffed, and wiped her streaming nose with the back of her hand.

George rolled his eyes. He reached into his pocket and took out his own grubby handkerchief. He made his sister blow her nose.

6 ADDIE'S HOMECOMING

Mother spent the next morning in a frenzy of cooking and baking for Addie's homecoming. She prepared a feast of beefsteak, brown gravy, green beans, canned peaches, baked cabbage, scalloped potatoes, stewed tomatoes, fresh bread, butter, and lemon raisin pie. The soddy filled with mouth-watering smells. Spread on the table was Mother's best white linen cloth. In the center stood a bouquet of fragrant pink prairie phlox and bright yellow puccoon that Nellie May had picked and placed in the old green glass sugar bowl.

"I hope we have enough room for everyone," Mother said. "Since Anna and Mr. Fency are coming, I think I'll set up another smaller table for Nellie May, Burt, and Lew. George, would you mind sitting with them?"

George ground his teeth to keep from exploding. He wanted everything to go smoothly for Addie's return. But his anger nearly overpowered him. To have to sit with the little children! Now that Addie was coming home, he was no longer the oldest. He was only one of the children again. How insulting! He did not answer Mother, hoping she would notice his moody silence and change her mind. But she was too busy arranging canned peaches in the rosebud china dish.

Reluctantly, George dragged the humiliating little table from the shed and set it inside the soddy.

"Kind of like getting ready for a preacher, isn't it, George?" Burt sniggered.

George did not reply. He did not want to lose his temper. Over the table he flung Mother's checkered tablecloth, the one with the worn spot in the corner. Buffalo slunk beneath the table to wait for Nellie's crumbs.

"Do you see Pa and Addie yet?" Mother asked Burt. "Her train was due in Defiance more than two hours ago. Where can they be?"

Burt peered out the window, trying to spot the wagon. "I don't see them. But there's another wagon coming. Looks like Anna and Mr. Fency, all dressed up."

Their neighbors the Fencys had been close friends, almost like family, ever since the Mills had come to Dakota. Since Anna and Mr. Fency had no children of their own, they showered George and his brothers and sisters with affection.

Mother untied her apron and hurried outside as Anna

climbed down from the wagon. "Hello!" Mother called merrily, and kissed Anna's plump cheek.

"Hello!" Mr. Fency boomed. He was dressed in a neat black suit and wore an old-fashioned stovepipe hat that made him appear even taller than he already was. "Well, where's the scholar?"

"She's not here yet," Nellie May said. She twirled around to attract everyone's attention. "How do you like my new sateen dress, Mr. Fency?"

"Very sublime. You look quite bedazzling!" Mr. Fency said, and winked. He turned to George and his brothers and shook hands with each of them. In a low, man-to-man voice he asked, "How are you gentlemen doing, all dressed up in your fancy duds? I don't know about you, but this stiff collar Anna forced me to wear is just about to strangle me."

Lew and Burt laughed. "You want us to unharness your horses, sir?" George asked.

"Why, that would be most helpful. But first I need to ask you something. Do you know the one about the inbound freighter and the outbound freighter?"

"No, sir, we don't," Lew said, elbowing Burt and grinning.

"Well, it seems there was this outbound freighter with four heavily loaded wagons going west to the Black Hills. The bullwhacker was Big Bad Bill. Bill could control six teams of oxen with just a six-foot whip and the sound of his voice."

"And what did Big Bad Bill say?" Burt asked, right on cue.

"He'd crack that whip and bellow, 'You great-big-stand-up-in-the-corner-and-bawl-for-buttermilk-when-you-know-there's-not-a-drop-in-the-house!' and those oxen would jump and zip like chained lightning." Mr. Fency slapped his knee the way he always did. "As I was saying, there was Bill, moving along minding his own business. All of a sudden he spots this inbound freighter coming east, right in his direction.

" 'Big Bad Bill,' says the bullwhacker on the inbound freighter, whose wagons are all empty now since the gold miners in the Black Hills bought everything he had, 'what yuh loaded with?'

"Bill says, 'Forty barrels of whisky an' one sack of flour.'

"Then the inbound freighter replies...,"

" 'What in the devil are you goin' to do with so much flour?' " the boys rang out, laughing the way they always did when Mr. Fency told a story. Mr. Fency laughed, too.

"Are you telling those innocent children that disgraceful story again?" Anna scolded.

"It's all right, Anna," George replied. "We know Mr. Fency isn't telling the truth."

"I never lie!" Mr. Fency insisted, smiling all the while. "Why, look who's coming! There's your pa and big sister."

Sure enough, George spotted his family's wagon. He waved. Addie waved back. As soon as Pa pulled close to the house, Addie jumped off the wagon, looking very sophisticated in her brown wool traveling jacket and smart little brown wool hat. She was smiling and crying at the same time as she ran to greet Mother, her sister, and her brothers. "Hello, Mother! And George and Lew and Burt and Nellie!"

"Hello, Addie," George said bashfully. His sister stood nearly as tall as Mother now. She had grown up so much; he felt as if she were a stranger.

"Hello, yourself!" Addie replied, and gave George a big hug. He was so embarrassed he just stood stiff as a fence post. "Hello, Anna and Mr. Fency!"

Anna dabbed her eyes with a handkerchief. She gave Addie a warm embrace. "Doesn't she look wonderful, Mr. Fency! Just like a lady."

"Yes, she does, my dear," Mr. Fency replied. He leaned over and respectfully shook Addie's hand.

"I want to see everything!" Addie said. She laughed and ran into the soddy. George, Lew, Burt, and Nellie May followed her. Addie examined the curtains, the stove, the cupboards, and Mother's geranium as if they were all fascinating objects she had never seen before. Then

she poked her head into the lean-to. "Just as messy as always, boys. Nothing has changed."

She darted outside. George and the others could barely keep up as she climbed onto the soddy roof. Then she scrambled down again and ran for the barn. Holding her skirt in an unladylike fashion, she hurried up the ladder to the loft, calling, "Come on, George! I got something to show you before the others catch up."

"I'm coming," George replied breathlessly as he joined his sister.

From her pocket she produced a folded paper. She handed it to George. "It's music for 'Pop Goes the Weasel.' One of the girls at school gave it to me," she said. "Since you're the musician in the family, I'm giving it to you."

George blushed. "The score doesn't look too difficult. Maybe I'll give you a concert." He hid the music in his pocket and grinned. Everything was going to work out just fine now that Addie was home again.

"Have you seen Tilla?" Addie asked about her old friend. "I wrote and told her I'd come to visit as soon as I could."

"Last time she stopped here was maybe two months ago. She brought one of her nephews. Ugliest baby I've ever seen," George said, and laughed. "She'll be glad to hear you're back."

"Mother says dinner's on the table!" Lew called from

the barn doorway. "Come on!"

George and Addie climbed down the ladder and hurried to the soddy. Reluctantly, George took his place with his younger brothers and sister at the little table. Addie sat with the grownups.

As soon as Pa had said grace, Mother passed around dish after dish of steaming food. George ate until he thought he would burst. Burt and Lew managed to keep up with him, refilling and emptying their plates just as quickly. Only Nellie May did not seem very hungry. She just sat, poking her lemon raisin pie with her fork.

"It's so wonderful to be home again!" Addie said. "Did you miss me, Burt and Lew?"

Lew grinned. "If I say no, will you go away and come back again tomorrow? I like these coming-home feasts Mother makes."

"Here, here!" Mr. Fency agreed. "Hurrah for the cook!"

Mother blushed.

"It was delicious, Becca," Pa said approvingly. He pushed back his chair and smiled broadly at Addie. "It isn't every day that a family gets to celebrate like this."

George looked around. Everyone seemed to be in a good mood. The time was perfect to make the announcement he had been practicing over and over. He cleared his throat and tapped his plate with a knife.

"George, is there something you'd like to say?" Mother asked.

"Yes," George said. He steadied himself, his hands on the table. "I have been waiting until Addie came home to tell you all."

"Tell us what?" Burt interrupted with a devilish grin. "That you're going to high school, too?"

"No," George said, trying hard not to let his voice falter. Out of the corner of his eye, he could see Pa crossing his arms in front of his chest. "I wanted to tell you all what I bought. It's a kind of investment, you might say."

Pa turned to Mr. Fency and Anna. "During the past year George and his friend made over forty dollars collecting buffalo bones and snaring gophers. Isn't that right, George?"

George nodded.

"Forty dollars is a lot of money, George," Mr. Fency said. "What did you do with your share of the loot?"

George gulped. Pa and Mother smiled as if they were both waiting for him to say something that would make them proud. George took a deep breath. "I bought a trombone."

"A trombone?" Mother said weakly. Her smile vanished.

"A trombone?" Pa leaned forward as if he hadn't heard correctly.

"That's right. I bought the trombone that Mr. Swain Finch had lent to me," George said quickly. He shot a beseeching glance at Addie. But his sister wasn't looking at him. She was looking with alarm at Pa. And Pa's face was growing redder by the minute.

"What do you mean you bought a trombone?" Pa's voice sounded cold and angry. "I thought you were going to buy something practical. Something like a good saddle horse. Something you could use."

"That's what *you* wanted me to buy," George said quietly, looking down at his plate so he did not have to meet Pa's fiery glare. "That's not what *I* wanted to buy."

"Well, now, shall we have some coffee?" Mother suggested, her voice bright and nervous. She stood up and began gathering the plates. "I'm sure we can settle this later. Anna and Mr. Fency did not come all this way to—"

"Twenty dollars is a lot of money, George," Pa interrupted. "A lot of money to waste on something like a trombone."

George looked at his father. He looked at Addie. Wasn't she going to say something? Wasn't she going to come to his defense the way he had hoped? "What do you think, Addie? Do you think a trombone is such a bad idea?"

Addie bit her lip. "I...I don't know," she stammered.

76

"George, this isn't the time for such a discussion," Mother said as if speaking to a disobedient toddler. "We can talk about it another time."

"Another time?" George crushed his napkin into a ball and slammed it down beside his plate. He turned to Pa and said as calmly as he could, "The trombone is bought and paid for, and it was my money."

"Is that so?" Pa's voice was rising. "I knew that money would burn a hole in your pocket. I knew—"

"Mother?" Nellie May said suddenly. Her face was flushed. "I don't feel so good."

Mother hurried to Nellie and felt her forehead. "My lamb, you're burning up! Come here and lie down. Addie, can you get a cool cloth for your sister? I'm afraid she has a fever."

Dinner ended abruptly with no more trombone discussion. George was relieved but watched anxiously as Anna knelt beside Nellie May and carefully examined her eyes. Anna had been a midwife before the Fencys came to Dakota, and she had taken care of lots of sick people. Gently, she pulled down Nellie's lower lid. The rim was angry red. Then she checked behind Nellie May's ears.

"Has she been coughing?" Anna asked.

"She's had a bit of a cold," Mother admitted. "What do you see?"

"Open your mouth, sweetheart," Anna told Nellie.

"Stand out of my light, will you, boys?"

George and his brothers took a step back. Nellie May opened her mouth. "They're sometimes hard to recognize," Anna said. "See by her back teeth—those white spots surrounded by redness? That's the first sign of measles. She'll probably break out in a couple days. Maybe as early as tomorrow."

"Measles!" Mother's voice cracked. "What should we do?"

George could tell Mother was afraid. He was glad Anna did not start talking in front of everyone about how the disease could be fatal. He had heard stories at school about how there was no medicine, no cure for measles. Orah May Hatch and Cora Ackley, two girls from town, had died from it less than a month ago. These thoughts terrified him.

"The farm will have to be put under quarantine. Nellie will need rest. We can darken the window so the light won't bother her eyes. Keep the room warm and give her plenty of water to drink. The rash usually lasts a couple days."

"A couple days," Pa said slowly. "What about the other children?"

"They will probably come down with it, too. We'll just have to wait and see. Have you or Becca ever had the measles?"

Pa nodded. "I have. What about you, Becca?"

Mother shook her head.

"Then you may catch it, too. The main thing that's dangerous about measles is the fever. The fever and complications," Anna replied quietly. "Don't worry, Becca. Everything will be all right."

Mother did not look the least convinced. Gently, she covered Nellie May with a quilt and ushered the boys outside. George lingered in the doorway. He watched Mother hovering over Nellie May and thought about the raggedy girl and the candy stick in Defiance. If only he had been more careful watching his sister that day, none of this would have happened! The measles were all his fault.

7 QUARANTINE

George sat miserably on the soddy's sole window ledge. He rested his chin on his bent knees and looked out at the blue sky. Twelve days had passed since Nellie came down with the measles. Now Burt, Lew, and Addie had spots, too. Outdoors, a balmy wind pushed hard against the windmill and sent it whirling. George would have liked to take a deep breath of the delicious early June breeze, but he knew he couldn't. No one was allowed to open the window. Fresh air, Anna said, was bad for measles.

George imagined big, fat bullheads swimming in bold circles down in Rattling Creek. But since he was supposed to stay indoors and help watch his brothers and sisters, he couldn't slip away to do a little fishing. Even if he were free to go where he pleased, he couldn't cross the Oak Hollow boundaries. The farm was under quarantine. Pa had said nobody could leave and nobody could visit, not even Shy.

The quarantine made George crazy with restlessness, as if he might explode through the walls at any moment. Being trapped indoors on a beautiful spring day was a hundred times worse than being snowbound during a winter blizzard. To make more room for the four mattresses that were left out all day for his brothers and sisters, the table, chairs, and cupboard of cooking supplies had been moved into the yard. Yet there was still hardly enough space to walk.

The soddy was dark and stuffy and smelled overpoweringly of the onion and mustard poultices that Mother applied to Nellie May's chest during the daytime to help her cough. At night the smell was worse. That was when Mother and Anna mixed warm turpentine and lard together and smeared it on Nellie May's chest. But her cough only seemed worse, and her fever would not go away.

George looked at his little sister. For once she lay unnaturally still, her rag doll in her arms. While Mother applied another damp cloth to Nellie's forehead, George turned away quickly and cracked his knuckles. If only he would catch the measles, too! Maybe then he wouldn't feel so terrible. Every morning since the epidemic had begun, he'd checked his face in Addie's hand mirror. Not one spot.

"Anna's outside cooking. George, when she's finished,

can you help bring in lunch for the children? They'll probably be awake soon," Mother said. She brushed a strand of hair from her worried, gaunt face.

"Lunch isn't boiled milk and bread again, is it?" George asked.

Mother frowned. "Yes, it is. And I don't want to hear any more of your complaints." She added softly, "Anna says boiled milk and bread is the best thing for getting back strength."

George turned toward the window so Mother couldn't see his disgusted face. Boiled milk and bread for breakfast, lunch, and dinner! The very smell of boiled milk made him gag, and he couldn't think of anything that tasted worse than limp, soggy bread chunks.

"She's making white weed tea. Bring that in, too, please," Mother reminded him as he tiptoed toward the door.

"Yes, Mother," George said, shuddering. The taste of white weed tea reminded him of the odor of horse manure. What could be healthful about something like that?

"And don't forget to close the door tight behind you."

"Yes, Mother." He sighed as he stepped outside, glad at last to escape from her endless orders and the smelly soddy. Outdoors he could breathe again; he could move around without stepping on someone.

"Hello, George," Anna called. She stood up stiffly with

the pan of milk she had been stirring over the fire. The smile on her face was only a shadow. There were circles under her eyes, just as there were under Mother's. Anna had not been back to her own homestead for almost two weeks. She had stayed at Oak Hollow around the clock to help take care of the children. Not once did she complain.

George felt another twinge of guilt. "Would you like me to give you a hand, Anna?"

"You can take the food in to our patients," she said.

"Did Pa send for the doctor?"

Anna poured steaming milk into five bowls. She carefully tore apart pieces of bread and dropped them in. "Your father left a note at the Fairchilds' for Shy to gallop to town. Shy's supposed to find Dr. McConkey and send him here fast as he can."

"I hope the man's sober," George mumbled. "I've heard sometimes he's so drunk he can't get on a horse." He frowned as he recalled other complaints about Dr. McConkey. "In town they say his only patients were horses and cows before he came to Dakota."

Anna sighed. "Well, maybe Dr. McConkey can at least bring us some quinine. Quinine would certainly help your little sister's fever."

"You think Nellie and the rest are going to be all right?" he asked, trying not to sound anxious.

"Your sisters and brothers are strong and they're young.

I've seen worse cases of measles before. We're doing everything we know how. God willing, they'll all make it."

"God willing," George repeated. But he still had his doubts.

Anna shooed away flies from the steaming bowls. "I'm worried about your mother. She hasn't had a wink of sleep in almost three days. I've tried to convince her to rest, but she won't. If she took a little nap out here in the shade, she'd feel stronger."

"I could keep my eye on the others in the soddy. That way you could get a nap, too."

Anna smiled. "You're a good boy, George."

He took the bowls inside. Addie, Lew, and Burt sat up and rubbed their eyes. "Mother, I'll make sure everyone eats," George said. "Since Nellie May's still asleep, why don't you go rest for a while? Anna says there's a nice shady place outside for you to take a nap."

"Are you sure you can handle everything, George?" Mother asked.

"Of course!" George replied. When Mother went outside, he passed out mugs of tea, spoons, and bowls of boiled milk and bread. As usual, no one was hungry.

"This stuff is what babies eat," Burt complained. He pushed the bowl away.

"Reminds me of dead dog guts," Lew said, mashing

the soggy bread with the back of his spoon.

"Anna made this special. So eat it and quit your griping!" George ordered.

"You're a rotten nurse, George," Addie said. "You're supposed to encourage your patients, not threaten them." She was sitting up, looking into her mirror. "What will I do if these spots never go away?"

"You'll probably have scars for life," Lew said cheerfully.

"No one will want to marry you, that's for sure, all pock-marked like a piece of bad cheese," Burt agreed.

"Addie, the lonely old maid," Lew added, "living in one of those tarpaper claim shacks out on the bluffs where nobody ever visits. Maybe you could raise sheep for company."

Addie picked up some bread and chucked it at Lew's head. Luckily, he ducked in time. Bread and milk splattered against the wall.

"Stop it!" George hissed nervously. If Nellie May woke up howling, Mother and Anna would come running. And then he would get all the blame.

"Burt and Lew started it," Addie said peevishly.

"How about some entertainment?" George interrupted. He hoped a distraction might stall a full-scale food fight.

Burt and Lew looked interested.

"I cannot think of anything you might do that would

be very entertaining," Addie said.

George sighed. What was wrong with Addie? Maybe measles had addled her brain.

"I want some entertainment," Lew said. "What harm will it do as long as we don't wake up Nellie May?"

"I just thought you might like to hear a tune," George said. "Something to take your mind off your measles."

"I wouldn't mind something to take my mind off boiled milk and bread," Burt agreed.

"Me, either," Lew piped in.

"Well, all right," Addie said.

George made sure that neither Anna nor Mother saw him as he hurried out of the soddy to the barn. He grabbed his trombone and ran back.

"What are you going to play?" Lew said eagerly.

George muted the trombone by stuffing the end with the burlap sack. He put the instrument to his lips. Softly, he played "Pop Goes the Weasel." Lew and Burt whispered the words:

> Around and round the cobbler's bench
> The monkey chased the weasel.
> The weasel stopped to scratch his chin.
> Pop! Goes the weasel!

For the first time in days, Addie smiled. "Play it again," Burt begged.

But before George could begin, the door opened.

"What's going on in here, George?" Pa demanded.

"I was just playing a little music...a little entertainment..." George mumbled.

"Entertainment? Well, put that thing away. Your sisters and brothers don't need entertainment. They need rest. Do you hear me?" Pa's face glowered.

George tried to hide the bulky trombone behind his back. "It was just a song Addie gave me. I was only trying to cheer—"

"You were only trying to make a nuisance," Pa replied angrily. "I have a good mind to ship that trombone back to Swain Finch for a refund."

"A refund?" George said.

Nellie May began coughing badly. "Mother!" she whimpered.

"Now see what you've done? Just a minute, I'll get your mother," Pa said to Nellie. "You hear me, George?" he warned in a low voice.

Pa went outside. George took a step back. His head throbbed. The trombone seemed so enormous. Where could he possibly hide it?

"I'm sorry, George. I didn't know a piece of music would cause so much trouble," Addie said softly. "Are you all right?"

"His face is kind of green," Burt said.

George slumped against the wall, the trombone under his arm.

Mother hurried inside. Behind her came Anna, who wrung out a fresh cloth and placed it on Nellie's forehead.

"Samuel just woke me," Mother whispered to Anna, as if the children couldn't hear every word. "He said Shy looked everywhere in town for the doctor. He even tried the saloons. But nobody's seen McConkey for two days."

"What's Samuel going to do?" Anna asked.

"He says he's going to ride to Scotland to see if the doctor there will come and help."

"That's twenty-five miles away! He'll never make it back by nightfall."

Mother bit her lip and stared anxiously at Nellie. "What if no one will come? What are we going to do?"

"We're going to hope and pray for the best," Anna replied.

"Mother?" George said. As he stepped forward, the floor seemed to buckle up beneath him.

"George, don't step on my arm!" Burt yowled.

Mother put her hand on George's forehead. She frowned. "George, you lie down on this bed."

"I can't lie down," George insisted. "I've got to put the trombone back in the loft where it will be safe."

"I'll take care of it for you, George," Anna said. "It seems you're going to join our other patients."

George did not know whether to feel worried or grateful. At last he would be just like his brothers and sisters. He lay down on his parents' bed and closed his eyes.

George was dreaming. Why else would Pa let him hold his gold pocket watch? Why else would Pa give him a whole silver dollar for no reason at all? George pressed the cool dollar and the pocket watch to each of his cheeks. When he pulled them away, the gold and the silver felt as hot as a stovepipe.

"Can someone please open the window?" he begged. "I can hardly breathe in here."

But no one seemed to understand him.

Music was coming from inside George's head. Low, reedy notes rollicked upward, lilting and lovely. "Play it again," he asked, "so I can remember it."

The melody repeated. This time it sounded more haunting, more beautiful. Was Pa listening, too? His face seemed so odd. It was melting. Why was Pa's face melting? George struggled to sit up for a closer look. But the music weighed against his shoulders, pinning him flat, filling the room with darkness.

8 FLY AWAY

George opened his eyes. His pillow felt damp, and his hair was soaked with sweat. Somebody was pressing a cool cloth against his forehead.

A voice said, "Be still, now."

"The fever broke?" another voice asked.

"Finally, yes."

Who was talking? Anna Fency and Mother. He lifted his head. He could see their worried expressions. Closing his eyes, he sank back in exhaustion. Why was he so weak? "Mother?" he said.

"Yes, dear heart?"

"Are my measles gone?"

"Not yet. Now try and take a sip of water."

George drank some water and went back to sleep. He thought he slept a very long time. When he woke up again, Anna and Mother were gone. It took him several minutes to get used to the blinding brightness around the edge of the closed curtain.

Across the room he saw Addie's rumpled brown hair above one coverlet. From another bed he heard Burt's snore. The two other mattresses were missing. Why?

Fear took hold of George, worse than the fever's chills. Something had happened. Something terrible.

"Lew?" he called desperately. "Nellie?" Maybe his brother and sister were well again. Maybe they were outside playing, just like old times. But George could not convince himself. Wasn't Lew the weak one? George remembered how Burt had jokingly predicted, "I bet Lew gets the worst case of measles of all five of us. Anyone want to lay a wager?"

George swung his feet out from under his blanket and tried to stand. The floor seemed to roll and pitch. *Thud, thud, thud.* A pounding noise echoed not far away. What was that sound?

"George, you aren't supposed to get out of bed!" Lew shouted. He stood in the doorway, carrying a basin of water. There were still a few scabs on his gaunt face.

"Where's Nellie May?" George demanded. "What's that noise?"

"Stay right there," Lew said quickly. He rushed out so fast that he sloshed water all over the doorstep.

When Anna appeared, her face was swollen, her eyes red.

"Mother didn't catch the measles did she? She's all

right, isn't she?" George asked. He felt frantic with worry.

Anna put her arm around George and sat down with him on the edge of the bed. "Your mother's all right," she said quietly. "It's our little Nellie May. She passed away last night."

"Nellie May?" George asked.

"Your sister died of pneumonia, the precious lamb. The fever from the measles just never let up. We did everything we could. Your Pa tried to get a doctor from Scotland. By then it was too late. The poor wee thing! At least now she's in heaven where there's no more suffering."

George could not believe it. There must have been some mistake. Not Nellie May. He felt as cold as if he were standing in a January wind. "...some don't survive in spite of everything we try," Anna went on. "That's just the way life is. It's God's will."

George wanted to shout, "You don't understand. What happened was *my* fault. I'm the one responsible."

But he said nothing.

The words trapped inside him twisted and writhed in his stomach like a poisonous snake. He tucked his hands under his armpits, but he could not stop his terrible shivering.

"Of course, your mother's taking this pretty bad," Anna said. "She hasn't left your sister even for a moment. We have her laid out real nice in the barn..."

The noise started again. *Thud, thud, thud.* George covered his ears so he did not have to listen. No matter how hard he tried, he could not keep out of his head that noise or Anna's voice.

Anna glanced toward the door. "Your father's been working all night on a fine oak coffin. Mr. Fency offered to help, but your pa refused. He said this was something he had to do all by himself."

Thud, thud, thud.

George lay back. He stared at the cheesecloth tacked across the ceiling. Pa had fastened that white cloth up there to keep dirt from falling into Mother's flapjack batter every time the children climbed on the sod roof to play. *Thud, thud, thud.* Nellie May used to jump up and down on that roof, harder than anyone.

"Why do you jump so wild, Nellie?" George had once asked.

"I mean to fly away," she'd answered.

And so she had.

George pulled the pillow over his head. Why her? Why not him?

"George?" Anna called, her voice sounding very far away. She patted him on the shoulder again. "It's all right to cry."

George did not answer. He rolled out of reach, his face against the wall.

Nellie May was buried that afternoon in a wooded spot along Rattling Creek. Since the farm was still under quarantine, the only people who could attend the service were the family and Anna and Mr. Fency. Pa said the Lord's Prayer. Mother and Anna sang "A Mighty Fortress Is Our God" and "Sweet By and By." At the chorus, Addie tearfully placed the red geranium on Nellie's grave.

"In the sweet by and by, we shall meet on that beautiful shore," Anna's thin, soprano voice rang out. "In the sweet by and by..."

George stared at the geranium and held on to Burt's shoulder. When the short service ended, he stumbled away, led by Burt as if he were a blind person. He could feel Burt's shoulder shaking as if he were sobbing, but no noise was coming out of his mouth.

"Burt?" George asked.

"Leave me alone!" Burt twisted free and ran toward the creek.

Mother passed by George, her black taffeta dress rustling. She did not say anything to him. She disappeared inside the house, followed by Addie, who was still crying. Pa, without changing his best Sunday clothes, hurried to the barn as if he had chores. And where was Lew? He was sitting atop the soddy roof. No amount of coaxing would persuade him to come down.

"Go away, George!" Lew called. Unable to think of

any place else to be alone, George fled and hid himself in the tall grass of the nearby field.

A week passed. Anna packed the small bundle of clothes Mr. Fency had brought for her. She hummed as she tucked a small Bible inside her carpetbag with the rest of her things.

"You're leaving?" George said, trying to control the tremor in his voice. It was silly, he knew. Anna had to go back to Mr. Fency and her own farm. She couldn't stay at Oak Hollow forever. And yet the idea of her leaving filled him with dread.

Anna smiled at George. "I have a garden that badly needs tending. Three new calves were born last week, and Mr. Fency can't take care of everything on his own." Gently, she lifted George's worried face in her hands. "You'll be all right. I have great faith in you."

George twisted free. He did not feel as if he would ever be all right again.

"You know you're welcome at our place anytime," she said, and clicked the carpetbag shut.

George nodded. He turned away before she could see his troubled face. Pa would never let him leave chores and field work just to visit. Mother had become so unreachable, so silent, it was as if she were sleepwalking. How could George explain that when Anna left Oak

Hollow, there'd be nobody to comfort him, nobody to listen?

"Goodbye, George," Anna said. "I hear your pa calling. Be a good help to your parents, will you? They need you."

"Sure," he said gruffly. "Goodbye, Anna." He hurried out of the soddy.

"You look well enough to help with milking today," said Pa. He stood in the yard, his arms crossed, scowling. Not once at the funeral had George seen his father weep. Not once. "Your brothers are waiting for you in the barn," Pa continued. "I can't be calling for you high and low every time there's work to be done."

"Yes, sir."

Pa's eyes narrowed. "I don't like your tone of voice, George. You mean disrespect?"

"No, sir." George squirmed.

"Get to work then."

Angrily, George snatched up a bucket. As he entered the cool, dim barn, he could hear his brothers arguing. A mourning dove called down from the rafters. George blinked. He half-expected to see Nellie May overhead in the loft, taunting, "Ha, ha. I fooled you!" George sighed. He knew nothing would ever be the same again.

"Come on, George," Burt shouted. "Don't see why I have to do all the work!" Burt sat at the milk stool, furiously milking Bess.

"What's the matter with Lew?" George demanded. His brother was crouched in the corner of a stall, sobbing, his hands over his ears.

"He won't listen to me. He won't do nothing," Burt announced. "Just comes in here and sits on a stool and says his stomach hurts and his head hurts and he can't milk. So I punched him."

George bent over his weeping brother. Before he could pry away Lew's hands from his ears to talk some sense into him, Lew jumped up and went screaming toward the house. "Why'd you go and do that, Burt?" George demanded. "All week you've got to hit somebody or break something. Don't you know we got enough troubles around here?"

Burt jumped to his feet, hands clenched. He knocked over the milk pail and lunged for George. The boys tumbled into the hay.

"Stop!" Addie shouted. She kicked and tugged and pulled apart her wrestling brothers. "I can hear you clear up at the house. Get off each other, right now!"

George staggered to his feet and wiped his bleeding mouth with the back of his hand. "He started it."

"I don't care who started it," Addie said angrily. "You're upsetting Mother with all your noise and fighting. Can't you get along for five minutes and give her some peace?"

George snorted. There was no arguing with his sister when she was in one of her high-and-mighty moods. Sullenly, he retreated to the loft. There, in the corner where he had told Anna to hide it so long ago, he found the burlap sack containing his trombone. How long had it been since he played a single note?

Carrying the sack, George climbed down the ladder and tiptoed outside. He stood in the shadow of the barn, where no one could see him. With the gleaming trombone to his lips, he played a song he made up as he went along, a song of sorrow and loneliness.

"What do you think you're doing?" Pa demanded.

George jumped at the sound of his father's angry voice.

"There's two pails of milk spilled, six cows bellowing, and you're out here playing that fool instrument." Pa took a step forward. His voice was steely. "Give it to me."

"Please...please, no. I won't play the trombone again where it bothers you. I promise. Only don't take it away."

"You've wasted enough time and good money on that thing. Tomorrow it's going back where it came from. When I go into town in the afternoon, I'm taking it to Swain Finch. If you won't ask for your money back, I will."

"But, Pa..."

"Pack the trombone in the bag. I've made up my mind. Tomorrow it's gone." Pa turned on his heel and headed for the calving pasture.

George slumped against the barn. He slid his finger along the shiny brass. The trombone was the most beautiful thing he had ever owned in his life. And it was his. He had earned it. Nobody was going to take the trombone away from him. Nobody. Not even Pa.

He could not stay here another day surrounded by so much sadness and anger. He could not bear to live another day under the same roof with his father, the tyrant. Tomorrow morning before anyone awoke, he would run away. He would flee Oak Hollow forever.

9 FOLLOW YOUR VISION

All night George tossed and turned, trying to come up with a plan. Where would he go? At last he remembered the one place he had felt genuinely happy.

Victor's big yellow tent. Why hadn't he thought of it before? He'd join the greatest traveling theatrical troupe west of the Mississippi! Jacob had said they were missing a trombonist. George sat up, filled with energy. He took his life's savings from under the mattress.

"There's no need to go alone," he told himself, and quietly crept out of bed. "Shy will come, too." It might be difficult to convince him, but he had to try. Shy had agreed to other schemes; why not this one? George took a deep breath. *Follow your vision. See where it takes you.*

Quickly, he scribbled a note and left it on the table. He tucked two loaves of bread under his arm and opened the soddy door. The sky was still dark. Stars shone. The air was cold and damp, but George did not notice. He pulled on his boots and hurried across the yard to the barn.

Something large and furry brushed against his leg. George jumped. "Get out of here, Buffalo!" he hissed. The dog paid no attention. He continued to happily lope along, tail wagging. George found a piece of rope and tied one end around Buffalo's neck and the other around the corral fence. But as soon as he started again for the barn, Buffalo began to whine piteously.

"You're going to wake everybody!" George whispered angrily, untying the rope. "Stay!" Without looking back, he ran into the barn, grabbed the burlap sack, and hurried away. He had to escape. No one could stop him. Not even Buffalo.

Over his shoulder George carried the burlap sack containing his trombone, the two loaves of bread, and all the money he had in the world—two silver dollars. He had been to the Fairchilds' farm so many times he knew his way even in the dark. As he approached, he could hear the bloodhounds howl. He wished that he'd brought along a stick. A big stick. Just in case one of the dogs decided to jump him.

"Get away!" he ordered, waving his arms at the six hounds who swarmed around him, leaping and sniffing. The friendly dogs boldly thrust their wet snouts all over his shoes and pants. The unfriendly dogs growled at something behind him. Their upper lips curled back, revealing sharp, menacing teeth. George turned.

"Buffalo!" he said with disgust. "Go home!" Buffalo crouched playfully and then bounded around the Fairchild shed with three barking dogs in pursuit.

"Shy, see what's riling the dogs!" Mr. Fairchild called sleepily from inside the dugout.

Shy stumbled through the door, hoisted up his overall straps, and scratched the back of his head. "Hullo, George. What are you doing here so early? Kind of cool weather for traveling with no coat."

"I don't need a coat," whispered George. Impatiently, he motioned for Shy to follow him away from the dugout, in case Shy's pa or one of his sisters might be listening. "I've got a very exciting plan—a real adventure. I'm running away. And I want you to come with me."

Shy looked at George in bewilderment. "You're running away? Where?"

"To join the Barrett Traveling Theatre. Come with me, Shy. Just think, we'll travel all over the world. I'm sure they'll hire me to play the trombone. And they could use somebody strong like you to help put up the tent. We'll have a great time. What do you say?"

"George, there's nowhere for you to run."

"What do you mean?"

"The theatre company is gone."

George was stunned. "Gone?"

"Yesterday while I was in town, I saw them packing up."

"Where...where did they go?"

"Jacob told me they were planning to travel west on the train to Chamberlain. As soon as they get to Chamberlain, they're going to cross the Missouri River, then head west on the road to Deadwood in the Black Hills. He said there are lots of paying customers in the gold camps."

George struggled to sort out these new facts. Slowly, his back straightened. He wouldn't give up. He couldn't. Deadwood. The Black Hills. Maybe this was where he and Shy were meant to journey. "We'll follow them," he said confidently, "on the next train out of Defiance. We can still catch up."

Shy took out his pocketknife and shredded a piece of grass. "What happens when you get to Chamberlain? What happens after you cross the river? You think you can travel on foot the whole way to the Black Hills? You know what it's like west of the river? My pa says that's the wildest, wickedest place on earth. You got to cross the Sioux reservation. You got to get past hostile Indians and outlaws coming from the gold mines. There ain't no towns, George. There ain't nothing except rattlesnakes and prairie dogs."

"If we stick together, there won't be anything to be afraid of. Come on. What do you say?"

"You don't have a horse. You don't have a gun. You got any food? You got any supplies?"

"I got my trombone, two loaves of bread, and two silver dollars in this sack, and—"

"It isn't going to work, George," Shy interrupted. He stopped shredding the piece of grass. "You're wasting your breath. Don't you see? I don't want to run away."

George gulped. He had always thought he could convince his best friend of anything. The belief that Shy would change his mind about staying on the farm had bolstered George's courage the whole way here. But now that he saw Shy's stubborn expression, he knew he had been wrong. Shy wasn't coming. "Why don't you want to escape from this place and see the world?" George persisted, suddenly furious that he had failed. "You scared?"

Shy sighed. "I'm not scared," he said quietly. "I have to help Pa. We've got forty more acres to plow this week. He needs me."

"Don't you see? A chance like this won't come again."

Shy shoved away a hound that licked at his ankle. He kept a steady gaze on the dogs racing back and forth across the field. "How come you're running away? You in trouble with your pa again?"

George cracked his knuckles. "Nope," he said quickly.

"I know you're all broke up about what happened. About your sister, I mean. And I feel real bad for you—"

"Forget it," George said. Shy's discomfort made him feel even worse. He wasn't ready to talk about his sister's death to anyone, not even his best friend. "I didn't come here to beg for sympathy."

Shy dug his toe into the ground. "Shoot, George, I know you're not begging for anything. All I'm trying to tell you is you're jumping into this too quick. Running away, I mean. Maybe you should go back home and think it over."

"I can't go back," George snapped. He recalled the note he had left:

Dear Pa—
I am going far away. I need to be on my own. I am taking my trombone. Do not come after me.
                              George

How could he face Pa after writing a note like that? "Shy," George said carefully, "I guess it was a plain waste of time to ask you to come with me."

Disloyalty! That accusation was the lowest blow George could have made, and he knew it. Shy's shoulders sagged. His face filled with hurt. "I guess I can't argue any sense into you."

"I guess not."

Shy shook his head as if he thought George had gone quite mad. "Just give me a minute, will you?"

"For what?"

"You'll see. I'll be right back." Shy disappeared into a nearby shed. When he returned, he had two awkward bundles, one under each arm. "Here," he said, shoving one bundle at George. "Twelve strings of gopher tails worth about five dollars when you cash them in at the dry goods store." He opened his fist. "Take these, too. It's just three silver dollars—maybe enough to help you buy a train ticket one way, at least."

"Shy, you just gave me all your gopher tails. I can't take your money, too."

Shy thrust the money into his hand. Then he held out the second bundle, a rolled horse blanket tied with a piece of rope. "Take this old blanket. It don't smell so good but my pa and me sometimes use it when we go hunting overnight. There's a tin of matches and an old canteen and a few pieces of dried jerky rolled up in there, too. And don't forget this." He held out his pocketknife.

"Can't take that."

"Take it." Shy placed the knife in George's hand.

George cradled the knife in the palm of his hand. He stared at the worn, black-horned handle and looked at his friend in wonder. Next to his brand-new repeating rifle, this was the most precious thing Shy owned.

"Well, I thank you," George said gruffly, and put the knife into his own pocket. Suddenly, he felt very frightened, very alone. There was no turning back.

"You better get going," Shy said, "before the sun comes up. I won't tell nobody I saw you or where you're going. Not even your pa. I give you my word."

George quickly wiped his eyes with his sleeve. Shy acted as if he did not notice. "I'd be scared if I was you," Shy said.

"I'm not scared. Nope," George lied. He shook his head and tried to smile. He was going all by himself. And he was leaving right now before he had another second thought. "When you catch Buffalo, send him home."

Shy gave George a friendly shove. George shoved him back. "Goodbye, George," Shy said softly. "Mail me one of those pretty color postcards when you get to Deadwood, will you?"

"Sure," George said. He stuffed Shy's rolled blanket and the bundle of gopher tails into his sack. Flinging the bulky bag over his shoulder, he trotted out to the road to Defiance. Even when he reached the road, he did not look back. He simply raised one hand, waved, and broke into a run.

10 WEST TO CHAMBERLAIN

"That'll be eight dollars and fifty cents for a one-way fare all the way to the Missouri River—the end of the line," the Defiance station master told George from behind the ticket window.

George counted out the five dollars he had received at the dry goods store when he traded in Shy's gopher tails. What good luck he'd had in finding the store open so early! He added his own two silver dollars and three dollars from Shy. Now all he had left was one dollar and fifty cents. "When is the next train, sir?" he asked, certain that the scowling, grey-haired man could hear his heart thumping wildly.

The station master poked a long, bony finger into his vest pocket and pulled out his watch. "Next train out of here rolls into town in fifteen minutes."

More good luck! In fifteen minutes he'd be on his

way. Pa would never catch him now. George couldn't keep from smiling. Everything was going to work out just fine.

"You know you got to change trains, don't you?" The station master polished his wire-rimmed glasses with his handkerchief.

George's smile disappeared.

"To get all the way to the river, you have to change trains at the Marion Junction," the station master explained.

"How...how do I do that?"

"When the conductor calls Marion, just get off at the platform and wait for the next west-bound train to Chamberlain. There's no other way to get to the river from here."

"Will I have to pay again?" George nervously fingered his remaining cash.

"No, just show the conductor your ticket. That will take you nearly 160 miles—to the last jumping-off place before Indian country."

"How far is Deadwood from Chamberlain?"

"About 280 more miles. But there isn't any train that goes to Deadwood, you know. You got to cross the river by ferry. West of the river you have to risk your scalp on the wagon road."

George stood as tall as he could. More than anything, he wanted to appear mature and capable, as if he took train rides and ferry rides by himself all the time. "Sir, by any chance did you see the Barrett Traveling Theatre buying train tickets here yesterday? I heard they're going on to Chamberlain, too."

The station master's eyes narrowed. "Why do you want to know?"

George bit his lip. "Saw some of their posters in town. I just wondered where they're going next, that's all."

"Can't trust those theatrical types," the station master replied. "Couple of them tried to sneak inside the baggage car so they wouldn't have to pay coach fares. Seems they thought nobody would notice them hiding with their costumes and scenery and wagon. How do you like that? Never heard such a caterwauling when I caught them and made them pay up." He slipped on his glasses and examined George critically. "You from around here, sonny?"

"No...no, I'm just visiting. I'm from out of town...Yankton."

"You sure look familiar."

George shook his head. "Never been here before." He picked up his sack and looked down the track. What if Pa came looking for him and the snooping station master told him which direction George was headed? He should never have mentioned the theatre company.

The station master leaned closer. "That your friend waiting for you over there?"

Good old Shy! George turned. But what he saw wasn't his best friend.

"Buffalo!" George hissed.

Buffalo rushed up to George, jumped up, and licked his angry face.

"Dogs can't ride the train. Railroad rules," the station master said.

"He's not...not coming with me," George stammered. He pushed the dog away with his foot. Now what was he going to do? Buffalo was ruining everything. "He'll go back home on his own. He's done it before."

"All the way to Yankton?"

George looked blankly at the station master. Then he blushed, remembering his own lie. "The dog doesn't live in Yankton. He's not my dog, see? He lives around here someplace. He just followed me. I've got to go. Goodbye."

He grabbed his sack and scurried around the corner of the station so he could hide behind a post on the platform. He felt like a fool, certain that the station master must be laughing at him. What if Pa came? The station master would tell him every stupid thing George had said. His escape was doomed. "Go on, get!" he snarled at Buffalo.

The dog was too interested in bits of stale bread and chicken bones that had fallen from travelers' picnic baskets to pay any attention. George prayed that the dog wouldn't knock someone over before the train arrived.

111

After what seemed forever, the enormous black steam engine bellowed into the station. Buffalo hid behind George in terror. Steel wheels squealed and screamed against steel track. The ground shook. Steam hissed. Smoke and cinders belched from the engine smokestack and littered George's clothing and Buffalo's fur.

"Go on home, Buffalo," George said in a stern voice. "Go on. Get!" The dog slunk away a few steps and paused, his tail tucked between his legs. He looked up at George with enormous, sad eyes. George bit his lip, hesitating. Maybe he shouldn't go. Maybe...

The train whistle shrieked. "All aboard!" the conductor shouted.

A man in a slick derby pushed past George. "You coming or going, sonny?"

George scrambled up the steps. He looked back once in time to see Buffalo slink under a baggage cart. George stumbled down the crowded aisle. So many faces, so many strangers—what if he couldn't find a seat?

"Watch that sack!" a toothless woman complained. She was perched between two huge carpetbags, peeling a hard-boiled egg into a dirty napkin on her lap.

"Sorry," George said. At last he found an empty spot. He slunk down into the worn upholstery, his sack on his knees. He closed his eyes tightly so that he could not look out the grimy window and see his dog on the platform.

Buffalo knew his way home. He'd be all right, wouldn't he?

There was a lurch, another jolt, and the train began to move. George opened his eyes. Defiance rolled past and disappeared. A tingle ran down his spine. At last, he was on his way! Nothing would stop him now.

The countryside flew by. New green grass glistened and rolled like waves in the wind. Sometimes he spied the flash of running water in a winding slough. Every once in a long while, he caught a glimpse of black plowed ground and a snatch of a tarpaper shack or a sod house with smoke coming from a stovepipe.

He thought of home. What was happening at Oak Hollow at that very moment? He tried to imagine his family's first reaction when they read his note and realized he was gone for good. Did Addie, Burt, and Lew already miss him? Did Mother weep? And Pa, what did he do?

George frowned. He did not want to think about Pa. To keep his mind off all the sorrow and anger he had left behind, he tried to count the buildings in each town he passed: Meno, Red Earth, Freeman, Lost Lake. When the towns had zipped past, he counted telegraph poles beside the track.

At Marion Junction he got off the train and waited on the platform, the way the station master had instructed. Because it would be an hour before the next train, he went to the little restaurant next to the station and spent fifty cents for a dozen sweet, sticky buns. The kind waitress filled his canteen with fresh water for free. George felt very grown-up as he made the wise decision to eat only half the buns and save the other half for later.

While he sat on the platform munching, he watched two red-haired boys who looked to be about Burt's age and a girl who seemed about the same age as Nellie May had been. They were arguing over who could sit on a battered trunk. A woman who appeared to be their mother dozed nearby. One of the boys finally shoved his taunting sister. She tumbled dramatically onto the platform, crying so loudly their mother awoke. "Leave your sister alone!" the mother ordered and gave each boy a swat on the seat of the pants. The little girl smiled with satisfaction and climbed back atop the trunk.

George remembered all the times he had wanted to beat up Nellie May for being stubborn and spoiled and ornery. He tried, but he couldn't take back those memories. After all, hadn't she deserved it? He sighed. With all his heart, he wished he had told Nellie May that he loved her. Now it was too late. He tucked a half-eaten bun back into the sack. He didn't feel hungry anymore.

The Chicago, Milwaukee, and St. Paul train barreled into the station. Westward to Chamberlain, the end of the line! He climbed aboard and found a seat. As long as he was moving, as long as he felt the rhythmic rocking and clicking of the swaying train, he wouldn't think about home or his family. He wouldn't think about Nellie May. He wouldn't think about anything except his glorious future as the best trombone player in the world—a performing musician in the Barrett Traveling Theatre!

Past Bridgewater, Alexandria, Mitchell, Plankinton, Kimball. The busy depots of the bigger towns seemed fascinating and exotic. He longed to shout and wave to everyone. George Mills was flying past on a marvelous adventure!

Hours went by. Never before had he realized what an enormous place Dakota was. Would he ever reach Chamberlain? When? The monstrous engine spewed more steam, more cinders. The train hurtled forever forward, rocking and clicking, clicking and rocking. At each stop, the stuffy, noisy passenger car filled with more people. All kinds of travelers, old and young, squeezed their way aboard.

There were families carrying crying babies and crates of chickens and loaves of bread and sacks of strange-smelling sausages. There were dreary-looking older men who sat alone and smoked. The younger men talked in loud, jolly voices and played cards. One man played tunes upon a harmonica that no one paid much attention to until he began "Home Sweet Home." The entire car became silent. Someone sniffled. George shifted uncomfortably in his seat.

"Enough of that!" a hard-looking man with a goatee interrupted. He blew his nose on a red handkerchief. "Give us something about the good country we're going to. You know the song that goes something like, 'Away, we're bound away, 'cross the wide Missouri'?"

The harmonica player wiped his mouth with his sleeve and nodded. Everyone in the train car seemed much relieved to hear him play "Shenandoah."

George gobbled the last of the sticky buns. In spite of the noise all around him, he nodded and dozed against the window, using his cap for a pillow. The man next to him snored, with a newspaper over his face.

"End of the line!" the conductor finally announced. "Everybody out!"

George woke up with a start. It was nearly twilight. He stumbled down the train steps, pushed along by the tide of passengers.

"Can you tell me how to get to the Missouri River ferry?" George called out to the conductor.

"Down the bluffs, that way. Only one road west out of town," the conductor bellowed. He was quickly swallowed up by a swarm of noisy fellows in fancy suit coats and shiny shoes.

Chamberlain was ten times bigger than Defiance—

bigger than any town George had ever seen. There was so much movement and noise it made him feel dizzy. He stared wide-eyed at the sea of strangers.

A pair of swarthy cowboys in spurs rushed past, knocking George against a miner wearing a wool shirt that smelled as if it had never been washed—or removed—in years. "Excuse me, sir," George said. The miner in the filthy shirt did not reply. He just kept walking.

The muddy main street, which stretched five blocks long, was lined with cheap wooden storefronts with signs nailed over the doors: Telegraph Office, Cottage Saloon, Bunch Grass Saloon, Drug Store, Bill Reece's Dance Hall, Macqueen Hotel, G. Andrews Dry Goods. Stray dogs, cattle, and teams of mules and horses streamed by. Homesteaders drove past in faded overalls, perched atop wagons packed with homesteading gear—plows, lumber, harnesses, barrels of food, and sacks of seed. Even though it was nearly evening, the whole town was wide awake and on the move. No time to rest!

A chorus of hammers echoed. Storefronts and houses seemed to be rising right out of the ground. Hurry up, now! Everywhere was bustling, impatient movement.

This was Chamberlain, the last jumping-off place before the Sioux Reservation.

"Need a ride to Deadwood?" a voice rang out.

"I'd rather ride to hell!" another answered.

A body exploded through the swinging doors of a saloon, barely missing George. The flying man landed face-down in the gumbo of Main Street. He didn't get up. Was he still breathing? Should someone do something? But when George turned and looked toward the saloon door, he could see bristly, grinning faces—faces that looked more like coyotes than men. Were they laughing at him? He hurrried on, holding tightly to his sack. How was it possible to feel so lonely surrounded by so many people?

Somehow he had to find the river. Which way was west? George stumbled along, pushed by the crowd. "Sir, can you tell me please, which way to the river?" he asked a man sweeping the boardwalk. The man pointed in the opposite direction. George began walking back the way he had come. Like a fish swimming upstream, he pushed his way through the crowd. What if he was too late? What if he got to the river and found the ferry wasn't taking any more passengers? He wiped the sweat from his forehead and kept trudging.

When he reached the outskirts of town, he could finally see the horizon again. That was a comfort. All about him were low hills, the rolling Missouri bluffs.

George quickened his step. The sun had set, and the sky was filled with a deep red glow. The river could not be much farther. He ran up the muddy road to the top of a bluff. When he looked down, the sight took his breath away. There was the Missouri, the widest, angriest river he had ever laid eyes on. Beyond, hidden in shadows, was the west river country—the wildest, wickedest place on earth.

11 WILDEST, WICKEDEST PLACE ON EARTH

George skidded down the muddy embankment past a driver and team on their way up. The driver swore and cracked a long bullwhip over his mules' heads, scarcely noticing George as he hurled past.

Where was the ferry? George searched the shoreline. He spotted a leaning tarpaper shack at the water's edge. Drifting close by was a crude flatboat, nothing more than a shallow box that looked to be about twenty feet long and half as wide, just big enough for a wagon and team of oxen. This must be the ferry the stationmaster had mentioned. There were no other boats to be seen.

Stretching across the river was a long cable that hung above the water and appeared to be anchored to a tall wooden post on either shore. The ferryboat was attached to the cable with its own rope, connected to an iron ring. The iron ring could slide on the cable all the way from shore to shore. A broad, muddy plank propped between the edge of the ferryboat deck and the shore served as a ramp. Inside the boat lay two long wooden poles and a trunklike box.

On the other side of the river, George could see a covered wagon waiting to cross. Struggling up the nearby embankment was a wagon and a driver, who apparently had just been ferried across the river. The driver paid no attention to George.

As George came closer to the shack, he could smell beans and onions cooking. He felt dizzy with hunger. "Hello! Anyone home?" he called.

The door flung open. Out stepped a short, stocky figure carrying a plate and a spoon. She shoveled the last of her dinner into her mouth and wiped her fingers on her patched, seed-sack skirt. She wore heavy work boots and a thick woolen military jacket. A sudden cool wind blew her grey hair every which way. She was frowning.

"Hello, yourself! I don't like to be interrupted while I'm eating," she grumbled. "It's almost closing time, but I see I've got another customer on the other side. You be wanting to cross, too? Where's the rest of your people?"

George was too surprised to speak. Weren't all ferryboat captains supposed to be men? "Yes, ma'am. I want to cross. I'm traveling alone."

The ferrywoman waved to the wagon waiting on the

other side of the river. "Toll costs three dollars."

"Ma'am, I haven't got that much," George admitted. If only he had resisted the temptation to buy all those sticky buns!

There was a sudden loud hoot from the man driving his team up the hill. "Don't try and cheat 'em, Keturah!" he called to the ferrywoman. "You just charged me fifty cents."

"Don't pay any attention to him. He just wants to run me out of business," Keturah said, licking her dinner from her fingers. Wrinkles wreathed her grey, mocking eyes. "How come you're crossing all by your lonesome? Without a moon, it's going to be dark as a mining shaft over there tonight. And in the morning things aren't going to get any better. Don't you know Sitting Bull and his warriors are still on the loose? It's dangerous Indian country on the other side."

George cracked his knuckles. "I'm not afraid."

"Aren't you a cocky fellow!" She opened her mouth and laughed, revealing very few teeth. "I'll wager you're running away from home. Could tell the minute I laid eyes on you."

George winced. Was he that obvious? "All I'm trying to do is catch up with the theatre company that came through here on their way to Deadwood. Did you see them? They're called the Barrett Traveling Theatre."

"I seen 'em all right. Their wagon and team came through early today. 'Course I don't ask no questions unless my passengers seem interested in jawing. But are you sure you want to join a crowd crookeder than a dog's hind leg?"

George nodded. He didn't believe a word she was telling him. All that mattered was that he wasn't far behind. "Will you take me across, ma'am? I can pay something."

Keturah looked him up and down, considering.

The aroma of hot beans made George's mouth water. There was still bread and jerky in his sack, but he knew that would have to last him until he found Victor. "How about a dollar for taking me across and giving me a plate of your beans? I'm powerful hungry."

The ferrywoman gave him a sly smile. "All right, it's a deal. I've got plenty left in the pot, lucky for you. You look like you're about to faint for lack of vittles. Way you're shivering, I'd say you was chilled to the bone, too. Should have thought to bring a coat before you run away. Going to be a windy night."

George shook his head. "I'm not a bit cold," he lied, embarrassed to seem so ill-prepared. He held his elbows tight against himself and clenched his teeth so they wouldn't rattle. He wasn't sure if it was the cool breeze or his own fear that was making him tremble.

Keturah disappeared inside her shack. When she

returned, she carried a gunny sack and a tin plate heaped with beans, onions, and a grisly slice of salt pork. He handed her all the money he had left. Twice she counted out one dollar before stuffing the money inside a sock in her pocket. She slung the sack on board the ferry.

"You can eat while I pole across. Put the plate on that box yonder while I untie the mooring," she ordered. "Hold the lantern aloft for me, will you? My eyes ain't too good in this dim light. Just do as I say and we won't capsize into the Big Muddy. Know how to swim?"

Reluctantly, George shook his head.

Keturah cackled. "Then I expect you'll be following my directions real careful!" She lit a lantern and waved it back and forth to signal the driver in the covered wagon on the other side that the ferry was coming across. "Hop on with those vittles. Don't forget your sack!"

George climbed into the boat and helped her haul the ramp on board. He held the lantern and watched her cast off the mooring lines. As soon as the boat was adrift, the current made it buck like a skittish horse. George sat down on the wooden box and began eating. He chewed and swallowed so quickly that he scarcely tasted anything.

Keturah carried what she called her "settin' pole" to the forward end of the ferry. There, she lowered the long, iron-tipped pole into the river. When the pole hit the river bottom, she leaned against it and walked slowly. As soon as the boat moved forward past the pole, she repeated the movement.

George wiped the plate clean with his finger. He took a swig of water from his canteen.

"Think you can handle a settin' pole, boy?" Keturah asked. "I could use a smoke."

George nodded. He took the pole and began inching the boat across. Now the river splashed gently against the sides of the ferry.

"River's running wilder than usual this time of year." Keturah sat on the wooden box and lit a corncob pipe. She took a puff and sighed. "Yes, sir. Worst flood since 1881. I seen a huge black bear on a cake of ice in early March. Tried to toss him a plank. All he did was dip his nose for a drink of water and float right on past. Heard somebody saw a bear on the Missouri all the way in Omaha. Could have been a different bear, I suppose."

George searched the growing shadows for floating bears —or worse.

The ferrywoman knocked the ashes out of her pipe. "There's trouble on the other side of the Missouri. And I'll tell you why. People are greedy. They want the Indians' land. The treaty gave the reservation to the Indians, but now the government wants the land back. Why are people always wanting what they aren't supposed to have?"

George did not know the answer to this. So he changed

the subject. "How long you been running this ferry?"

"Five years by myself. Before that, my man helped me. Then he got restless and went out West to prospect. Expect he'll be crawling home any day now, if he doesn't lose his scalp first. You sure you don't want to turn back? Don't mean to insult you, but do you know what happens to folks stupid enough to go on foot west of the Missouri with no horse and no gun?"

Without pausing to hear his answer, she continued, "They get robbed. They get scalped. They get their throats slit. They get left for vultures. And that's if they're lucky."

George's palms began to sweat. He had no money left. Even if he wanted to go home, he couldn't pay the fare to cross the river again. Clearly, Keturah didn't ferry anyone for free.

"What are you carrying in that sack, boy?"

George hesitated. Would she rob him?

"Cat got your tongue? What's in there—gold?"

"A trombone, that's all."

"A trombone!" Keturah slapped her leg. "Now I've heard everything! A trombone won't defend you against a scalping knife."

George squirmed.

The ferrywoman stood up. "Hand me the pole. I'd like to hear a tune. What'll you play for me?"

"I...I don't know. How about 'Pop Goes the Weasel'?"

George pulled out the trombone. Straddling the bench, he put the instrument to his lips.

Bright, lilting music echoed over the dark water.

Keturah tapped her foot and grinned a toothless grin. "That's a grand song—'Pop Goes the Weasel.' Now it's my turn to give you something. Take a look see in that gunny sack yonder."

When George reached inside the sack, he felt something soft.

"Pull it out!" Keturah exclaimed. "Ain't going to bite."

Gingerly, George removed a dark green, thick wool jacket. Its smell was overpowering. He tried not to breathe.

"Got skunked, but there's nothing wrong with it," she insisted. "Will keep you warm."

George knew skunk smell was nearly impossible to get rid of. It had taken months for Buffalo to lose the awful odor after he had tangled with a skunk hiding in the barn. George wanted to chuck the jacket overboard. But he didn't want to insult the ferrywoman. "Thank you," he said politely. He folded the jacket and placed it near his feet.

"We're almost there," she said. "You know, whenever you want to come back, just come to shore and I'll ferry you across. Won't have to pay me nothing. Just play that tune again."

"Oh, I won't be coming back, ma'am," George said.

"You never know," she said. The ferry bucked and plunged. George grabbed his sack; with his other hand, he gripped the bench. Keturah thrust the pole into the water. The ferry bumped and ground against the muddy bank.

George tossed the mooring rope to the waiting wagon driver. The driver tied the rope securely to the tall wooden post. "Hello, Sugarplum," the man called to Keturah. "Some fancy music you're making these days."

Keturah spit contemptuously and threw down the gangplank. "Take a lot more than sweet-talk to pay me for crossing you in the dark, Hank."

"Well, I'm sure not going to pay you no three dollars, you old river pirate."

"Better get on board," Keturah answered, "before I leave you stranded. Don't forget the jacket, boy. You're going to need it."

George jumped to shore with his sack and the smelly coat. The driver guided his uneasy team and wagon over the gangplank onto the ferry. The gangplank was lifted and the mooring untied.

Keturah stood poised with her pole pushed against the bank. "Boy!" she barked. "Don't wander off the wagon road or you'll be lost in dry hill country. And watch for snakes and keep your eye out for the White River. After that comes the Badlands. They don't call it hell with the fires burnt out for nothing! You hear me?"

"I hear you, ma'am! Goodbye!" George waved. The bobbing ferry lantern grew fainter. Overhead there were no stars, no moon. Darkness had swallowed him. He was alone—all alone.

Every way he turned he heard the woeful lapping of the Missouri and smelled the dank odor of ancient, water-soaked wood and silt. And skunk. Disgusted, George dropped Keturah's coat on a large, flat rock. He shivered. What now?

Build a fire. But would the twigs and driftwood along the shore be dry enough? He inched carefully along the river, fumbling on the ground for wood. He threw down soggy branches and kept searching until he found four fairly dry branches and a handful of twigs. He headed back to the place where he had left the rest of his belongings. He was doing just fine on his own, just fine. In a few moments, he'd have a warm—

Splash! He stumbled head over heels, landing in a shallow pool of cold water. The sticks flew. George sat up, sputtering and soaked to the skin. He wiped something slimy from his face. He stomped out of the pool, dripping and angry. His dry firewood was gone. His boots were soggy. His teeth chattered. Thank goodness the matches and food were still safe and dry.

Something rustled in the underbrush. George held his

breath. He gazed hard into the darkness. Might be anything—a thirsty deer, a fox. Or maybe something bigger—something with sharp teeth. Maybe a wolf.

He broke into a stumbling run. He tripped over a rock, hollering and waving his arms to frighten the animal away. What if it was nosing through his sack, eating all his food?

He fumbled along the shore, searching for the rock where he had left the sack. Where was it? His hand brushed something. At last! He reached inside the blanket roll and found the tin box of matches.

His hands shook as he felt for the rough edge along the top of the box. He used this to strike the match. Nothing happened. *Do not panic!* He tried again. Light! His blindness gone, he cupped one hand around the match. He held the light up, looking toward the bushes. He saw nothing.

The flame flickered and sputtered out. One precious match was gone.

He had to think. What should he do? Shivering, he squatted on the rock, his arms wrapped around himself. He would never get warm in these wet clothes. If only he had something dry and warm to wear. He sniffed. Keturah's jacket! He pulled it on over his soggy shirt. The odor made his eyes water, but he at least felt warmer.

Again, he crept a short distance from the rock. Again he felt along the bank, searching for dry wood. He was aware of every sound, every movement. A bush shook.

"Go away!" George shouted with all his might.

"Away...away...away...," the river echoed.

The air filled with the distinctive, high-pitched scream of a raccoon. There was a sudden frantic thrashing and then silence. As George breathed a sigh of relief, he again became aware of his coat's powerful odor. Had the smell of skunk scared away the intruder? George smiled, feeling a little more hopeful. Soon he would have a fire. He would eat something. He would sleep. Everything was going to be all right.

At last he found a few sticks that seemed to be dry. He returned to the flat rock and carefully arranged the wood. He lit a second match. Hands shaking, he held the match to the wood.

The flame flickered and sputtered out.

"Don't you know the wood's green?" he heard Pa's voice scold.

Shivering and miserable, George gripped the dead match between his fingers. Did he dare waste any more? Until he found Victor and the theatre company, he had to use as little of his supplies as he could. Exhausted, he abandoned the plan to build a fire. He'd just curl up and try to sleep.

To ward off the chilly, damp night air, he wrapped the ferry woman's jacket and Shy's musty blanket around himself. If he had Buffalo with him, he wouldn't feel so alone. He remembered how Buffalo had warmed their feet when he and his brothers slept in the barn. George wiggled his toes in his cold, wet boots. He tried not to think about Buffalo's thick, warm fur. With his head on the scratchy sack, he closed his eyes. In only a few minutes, he was lulled asleep by the steady warning chant of the river.

He dreamed of black bears.

12 ON HIS OWN

With the first morning light, George uncurled. His head ached, his legs felt frozen stiff, and his clothes were damp. Bewildered, he sat up. Where was he? He remembered: he was on the Missouri River, and he was running away.

He stretched. A thick, grey mist covered the river. The town of Chamberlain and the east bank had disappeared completely. He might be anywhere—another country far, far away. The shrouded river and bluffs, the ghostly trees— everything looked mysterious and forbidding.

He rubbed his eyes. Well, at least he had survived his first night alone. That was something, wasn't it?

He checked to make sure his trombone was all right. Now that it was light, he felt better. When he had finished eating the tough, salty jerky and half a loaf of bread, he rolled up his blanket and stuffed it in the sack. He splashed muddy, brown Missouri river water on his face. Then he refilled the canteen.

Slinging the sack over his shoulder, he loped up the rutted wagon road that wound through the bluffs. Which of these wheel marks belonged to Victor's wagon? He examined a fresh trail. Maybe this one. Just thinking about finally catching up with the Barrett Traveling Theatre made him quicken his pace.

From among the willows, birds piped and chattered encouraging songs. He had made his way by foot, by train, and by ferry. And look how far he had come! Everything would turn out fine. As long as he kept moving and concentrating on new places, new people, he wouldn't have time to think about Oak Hollow. The journey was all that mattered.

Another half mile along the wagon road, the trees thinned out. The mist lifted. Now he could finally see the west river country—windswept, with scorched patches of prickly pear cactus and stubby buffalo grass. Nothing like the luxuriant bluestem grass that grew back home. Why, there were places along Rattling Creek where the grass was so tall, he could hide in it on horseback.

Don't think about home. Keep walking.

George hurried along, his sack banging against his back. The grass grew even thinner. In many places, hard-baked gumbo lay cracked and exposed like an open sore. Restless wind devils flung sharp dust into the air. Prairie dogs darted across the road, diving into countless cone-shaped burrows. He had never seen so many of the yellow snub-nosed creatures. They whistled shrill warnings. What were they trying to tell him?

Ahead he saw no homesteads, no windmills, no fence posts. Not one sign of another living soul. Only the road stretching ahead for miles, clear to the horizon. He tried to fix his eye on some point on a far rise to mark his progress as he walked. But with each step, he felt no closer to his goal. The prairie's vastness confused his sense of distance.

Keturah's voice mocked him. *"You crossing all by your lonesome, boy?"*

"West of the river, you have to risk your scalp on the wagon road," the ticket agent called to him.

He stopped watching the horizon and focused instead on the next clump of coneflowers. As he walked, he hummed "Pop Goes the Weasel"; then he made up new words and sang those, too. But it was lonely singing all by himself with only the wind for company.

What would Shy do if he were here? He would certainly have been able to start a fire last night and keep it going. Well, George decided, if he did not catch up with the theatre company by tonight, he'd rig up a spit with sticks and start a proper fire himself. Then he'd snare himself a nice, fat jackrabbit, clean it with Shy's pocketknife, and cook it. Why, he and Shy had made the same dinner countless times when they wandered along the Jim River back home. There was nothing like the taste of tender, roasted rabbit. George licked his lips.

He put his hand into his pocket and held the knife. It was reassuring just to have it there. Of course, he couldn't talk to a knife the way he could talk to Shy. George felt a lump rising in his throat. What if he never saw Shy again?

Don't think about Shy. Keep walking.

He plodded on. Again he studied the horizon. No sign of a wagon, no sign of anyone. Whenever the road circled around an old buffalo wallow or disappeared down a dry creek bed, he hurried faster. Losing sight of the horizon made him nervous. On the next rise he half-expected to find Indians or outlaws waiting in ambush. As soon as he could see the horizon again, he felt better, but only for a moment. Then he began to worry about the next dip in the road. In the warm sunshine, his pants began to dry. He took off the coat and flung it over his shoulder so his shirt could dry as well.

When the sun was directly overhead, he finally rested. He sat beside the road and ravenously ate the rest of the bread, even though he knew he should save part of it. What if he couldn't catch a rabbit that evening? What if he didn't reach the theatre wagon until late tomorrow? He would have to go hungry. His head understood this, but his stomach did not. He could still hear his belly growl as he drank from the canteen.

Time to move on. He stood up and brushed the seat of his pants. He pitched a rock at the fat prairie dogs that roamed nearby. They dove out of sight. "Farewell!" he called.

All afternoon, the delicious idea of cooked rabbit crowded his thoughts. But the dream of dinner could not quite keep his mind off his aching feet. When he could no longer stand his hot, squeaking boots, he pulled them off. He flung them over his shoulder and walked barefoot in the soft spots along the side of the road. That was better!

Suddenly, he heard a shaking song that turned his mouth dry as cotton.

Buzzzzzzzzzzzzz!

A shape paused, then flashed between tufts of grass. *"Watch out! Watch out!"* an eerie voice hissed.

Who said that?

Sweat trickled down the back of his neck and the insides of his arms. Why had he taken off his boots, leaving his feet bare and unprotected?

"Help!" he shouted. "Somebody help me!"

"Me-me-me-me," his echo answered.

George stood motionless, his eyes squeezed shut. After what seemed a very long time, he opened his eyes and searched all around him. The snake was gone. Had he only imagined it?

Unwilling to take any chances, he pulled his socks and boots back on. He would never again take them off on the road. Never.

He kept walking. The sun was dipping so that bright rays shone directly into his eyes. He blinked. Soon it would be dusk. His stomach rumbled, and he knew that if he was going to catch a rabbit, he'd have to move fast. In the long shadows of late afternoon, rabbits came out of hiding to search for food.

In the distance he saw a grove of trees and a long stretch of grass. Where there were trees, there was water. *"Don't leave the wagon road,"* Keturah had told him. But what else could he do? Perhaps he was near the White River. And maybe he would find a place to spend the night.

Trudging through the rustling grass, he listened again for the fearsome, low warning of another rattler. Only courage and hunger drove him on. Beyond a cutbank, he discovered a shallow ravine. At the bottom was a small stream bordered by a grove of cottonwood trees and spindly willows.

He sat down under a big cottonwood, his sack beside him, and looked up into the budding branches. The enormous tree seemed comforting. He bent over the stream, took a long drink, and splashed water on his face. Now it was time to find dinner.

George crept along the stream, as he and Shy had done so many times along Rattling Creek. He searched for telltale jackrabbit tracks in the mud—clues leading to the places jacks hid, under bushes or inside abandoned badger holes. When he found several well-traveled paths, he unraveled three yard-long pieces of hemp from the rope that had bound the blanket roll. Skillfully, he tied each into a lasso. He draped each noose to hang above the rabbit tracks about the height of a jack's head. The running end of each snare he secured to strong branches.

As he returned noiselessly to the big cottonwood, he heard a proud red-wing calling, "Konk-la-ree! Konk-la-ree!" Dry leaves rustled. The creek bed was alive with golden plovers, croaking toads, and swooping swallow-tailed kites, all searching for food. Surely there would also be plenty of nice fat jackrabbits looking for dinner, too. George hoped that the rabbits would not see the snares in the dim light.

Seated beneath the cottonwood, George whittled sharp ends on a straight stick. He gathered up a pile of brush, dead moss, grass, and some larger branches. Now all he needed was a rabbit. He leaned against the tree and tried not to fall asleep. But his eyes refused to remain open.

What was that?

He snapped awake. He sensed movement in the deepening shadows. Someone was watching him. An Indian? An outlaw? He flicked open the pocketknife.

"Who's there? Come out!" he shouted, jumping to his feet.

"Who?" a terrible voice answered.

Something rustled in the underbrush. Eerie red eyes blinked. George raised the knife, his entire body poised, ready to strike.

Swoosh! Something soft and terrifying fluttered past his upraised arm. It soared into the deepening sky and disappeared, like a laughing angel on wing.

Nellie, is that you?

A sudden breeze rocked the big cottonwood.

Nellie, answer me!

Branches creaked.

You can buy me a candy stick, all right, George? I want a red cinnamon kind.

The hair on George's arms stood on end. He sat still, unable to speak or move, filled with fear and longing. But all he heard was the wind and the hoot of an owl.

He sighed. Only an old owl! His empty stomach was making him react like a fool. Well, he had better keep his wits about him or he would soon be even hungrier. Taking a deep breath, he made his way silently back along the creek to check the snares. The first trap was empty, but the hemp had broken. Wasn't it strong enough to hold a jackrabbit?

The next snare appeared untouched. Maybe there were no jackrabbits around here. Maybe he should have clobbered one of those prairie dogs when he had had the chance. Roasted prairie dog would have tasted better than nothing.

Hope nearly gone, he continued on to the last snare. He could hardly bear to look. He pushed away willow branches and saw a limp young jackrabbit.

With a sense of joy and relief, he carried his catch back to his campsite. There he quickly started a fire. With Shy's knife he went to work, slitting the back of the rabbit's neck and pulling away the skin as easily as if he were slipping off a glove. Then he chopped off the head and the feet, slit between the ribs, and shook out the insides. He skewered the cleaned rabbit on the sharpened stick which he hung between two forked branches over the fire. Yes, he had done a good job. Even Shy would have agreed.

Carefully, he turned the rabbit and cooked each side brown and crisp. The ravine filled with the delicious aroma. Overhead, the pale lavender sky turned deep purple. He looked up at winking stars. Another day on his own. And he had survived. Certainly, he could survive tomorrow, too.

13 A MEMBER OF
    THE COMPANY

When George awoke in the cool grey dawn, he thought he heard singing. He listened. Nothing. His stomach felt empty again. He took a swig of water from the canteen. But instead of soothing the grumbling, the water seemed only to make his hunger worse. Closing his eyes, he saw a table spread with one of Mother's wonderful breakfasts— fried potatoes, flapjacks, and hot biscuits and gravy.

Mustn't think about home. He opened his eyes and struggled to his feet. The theatre company could not be too far away now. He had to keep moving. Quickly, he rolled up his blanket.

When he reached the road, he paused, listening. Yes! From someplace not too far away he recognized the faint, unmistakable sound of someone practicing scales. "Do-re-me-fa-so-la-ti-do! Do-ti-la-so-fa-me-re-do!"

George headed toward the sound.

"Do-re-me-fa-so-la-ti-do! Do-ti-la-so-fa-me-re-do!"

A chorus of off-key soprano voices rang out, louder now. He broke into a run. Around the next bend, he spied a wagon pulled off the road. There was no team in sight. A sign on the white canvas said: "Barrett Traveling Theatre."

"Victor! Jacob!" George shouted joyfully as he hurried closer.

Where was everyone? A campfire smoldered. Steam rose from a blackened pot of coffee set on a rock. A wooden spoon lay in the dirt. George touched the kettle of gruel beside the fire and quickly drew away his hand. It was still hot. "Hello?" he called. "Anybody here?"

"Put down that sack and stick your hands in the air!" a voice warned.

George spun around in time to see the long barrel of a gun poke between the wagon flaps. He dropped the sack gently on the ground. "I'm no outlaw," he shouted. "My name is George Mills, and I came all the way here with my trombone to join your theatre. I've been following you for two days and two nights. If you'd just let me play for you—"

"Leave that sack alone. How do we know you don't have a gun in there? Keep your hands up!" The flaps parted, and an angry, red face shot into view. The actor climbed out of the wagon and circled George, holding the gun at his head. "Whoooweee! You stink!"

George blushed with embarrassment.

The actor lifted a dirty, red handkerchief to his face. "Move and I blast your head off."

"Help, Horace!" a woman screamed.

The wagon teetered as a wheel buckled and collapsed into pieces. Crash! A plump woman in a red dress tumbled out. She was followed by a shrieking blonde woman. The actor who George remembered was called Steele dove out next.

"Now what's the problem?" shouted Victor, who suddenly appeared near the campfire. Behind him trudged Jacob, leading two horses. Jacob's face was streaked with sweat, and his clothes were dirty and torn. George started toward them. He stopped when he felt the rifle poking between his shoulder blades.

"That wagon! See how the wheel fell apart?" the blonde woman shrieked. She kicked the pile of broken spokes and the loose tire rim. "We were almost killed!" She shook her head so vehemently that her curls bounced.

"Anybody hurt, Blanche?" Victor asked. "You all right, Estelle? How about you, Steele?" The actor and actresses brushed themselves off and glared at George.

"It's his fault," Horace said, poking George in the back again. "Just take a whiff. You know what they say about skunks. They bring bad luck."

"And he *is* wearing a green coat," Steele agreed.

"I would never think of tempting fate by wearing a green coat."

George felt his face burning.

"Please, no more of your superstitions," Victor said. "You act as if a peacock just ran into camp."

"Don't even say that word. Don't even *think* that word," Horace said between clenched teeth. He mumbled an incantation and twirled around twice with his fingers crossed.

Jacob laughed. "You sure frighten easily for someone who is famous for leaping through vampire traps and flying to heaven on mere wires!"

Horace scowled.

"Put the gun down," Victor said gently, "and tie these fine steeds to the back of the wagon where they will not escape again. Is breakfast ready? I'm famished."

"Sir?" George said. "Can I put my hands down now?"

"Certainly, certainly," Victor replied. He picked up the wooden spoon, blew off the dirt, and gave the grey gruel a stir.

"I remember you. You're the boy from that town with the ridiculous name," Jacob said, keeping his distance as he inspected George. "What was it?"

"Defiance," George replied in a small voice. His knees felt strangely rubbery. What were those small black specks flying past his eyes?

146

"Dreadful place," Jacob said. "You all right? Maybe you better sit down. Your face is as pale as Banquo's ghost."

"You may quote *Hamlet* all you like," Horace grumbled, "but never, never, never mention one word from that Scottish play."

Victor sighed. "I am very fond of *Mac*—"

"Stop!" Horace cried. "Do not speak another word."

Banquo? Hamlet? Scotland? George did not know what Jacob and Horace were talking about. He sat down on a rock with his head between his knees until the faintness went away. Wasn't anyone going to give him some food? Wasn't anyone going to ask how he got here? Weren't they going to ask him anything?

Finally, Victor spooned up bowls of gruel. "Young fellow, this first breakfast goes to you."

George took the bowl. "Thank you, sir." He lowered his eyes so that he did not have to meet the hungry, accusing stares of the rest of the theatre company. When his family invited a guest to dinner, they waited until everyone was served before eating. He held his bowl protectively in the crook of his arm, waiting for Victor's signal to begin.

"Take your turns, please! Remember, this is the last of our grub," Victor shouted. Estelle, Blanche, Horace, Jacob, and Steele pushed each other and snatched bowls and spoons. Their fierce elbowing reminded George of schoolchildren rushing to recess.

"Out of my way!"

"That bowl's mine!"

"No, it ain't."

"I'm here first."

Horace and Steele did not bother to sit down to eat. They held their bowls close to their faces and slurped noisily. As soon as Victor moved away from the pot, they scraped out every last bit. There was neither milk nor sorghum syrup for the gruel, which tasted burned. When George had finished every speck, he still felt hungry. But he knew there was no more.

"When we going on, Boss?" Steele asked. He tossed the bowls into the blackened pot and poured in a bucket of dirty water.

"As soon as we get that wheel fixed," Victor replied. "We've lost a lot of valuable time chasing horses. And now we must make repairs. Luckily, we've got a spare wheel. I only hope it doesn't fall apart, too."

"Ain't my fault," Horace grumbled. "*Someone* was whistling in the dressing room." He glared at the actress in the red dress.

"I wasn't whistling!" she insisted.

"Blanche, I heard you plain as the nose on my face. That's why I told you to go outside, turn around three times, knock, and wait to be invited back in. But did you do as I said? Did you even try to cancel out the bad luck? No, you did not."

"Ain't my fault!" Blanche howled. "It's his fault!" She pointed at George. "He's the one in the green skunk coat."

Victor sighed. "No one said the broken wagon wheel was anyone's fault. We will all rise to the occasion and make the best of the situation. Isn't that right, Estelle?"

Estelle's rouged cheeks wrinkled in a frown. "What are we going to do about the kid?"

They were all staring at him again. George felt as if he were shrinking.

"He says he's got a trombone. He says he wants to join up." Steele sniggered.

Victor smiled at George. "A musician seeking an audition all the way out here? Now that's what I call ambition. Tell me, son, what's your name?"

"George. George Mills, sir."

"That your stage name or your real name?" Blanche taunted. She laughed with a high-pitched shriek. Victor gave her a threatening look, and she shut her mouth.

"George Mills is my *real* name," he said. "Sir, I met you in Defiance, do you remember? You let me and my friend watch a rehearsal for *King Lear*. It was the best thing I ever saw in my life."

"I *am* a magnificent Lear, that is true. I can show you newspaper reviews. 'To see Garbanzo act is like reading

149

Shakespeare by flashes of lightning.' " Victor beamed with pride. "Hamlet, Macbeth, Lear. I've played them all brilliantly—of course."

Estelle rolled her eyes. Blanche, who was busy picking her teeth, paused to make a disgusted face.

Jacob turned to George. "Is it true that you have your own instrument?"

George quickly reached into his sack and produced the shining trombone. He wiped it carefully with his shirttail and played a quick scale before he handed it to Jacob. "Cost me twenty dollars."

"Twenty dollars?" Jacob said. "Nice tone. Very nice."

George could see that the other actors and actresses were impressed, too. They winked and nudged each other.

"Let's hear you play something," Jacob said, giving the trombone back.

George put the trombone to his lips and played a rousing version of "Wait for the Wagon."

Victor clapped. "Excellent! Do you know anything by John Philip Sousa?"

George bit his lip, embarrassed that he had never heard of Sousa. "Maybe if you sing one of his songs, I can play it back."

Jacob hummed a complex passage of rising and falling notes. George mimicked the melody on the trombone.

"Bravo!" Victor said. "You have a splendid ear."

George blushed. "What I want to know, sir, is will you let me come with you?" He hoped he did not sound too rude and eager, but he was so very anxious. "I'll work for nothing. I don't need a salary."

"Salary!" Steele said, and snorted. "I'd like to see a salary myself one of these days!"

"All I ask is meals and a place to sleep," George begged.

Victor folded his arms. "You know anything about horses?"

"Yes, sir. Pa..." George's voice broke slightly. He cleared his throat and started again. "My father has one of the biggest outfits of horses and cattle and mules in Hutchinson county. I used to help take care of them."

"Know anything about wagons?" Victor asked.

"I know a bit. Enough to replace a wheel."

Victor smiled. "All right then. You're hired!" He clapped his hands. "Players, in no time at all we will be ready to roll onward to glory!"

No one offered to help George unload the wagon. No one volunteered to help him search the nearest creekbed for a long, sturdy branch. He used the branch and a barrel to create a makeshift lever under the wagon. "Is anybody going to lend a hand? I'll need everyone's weight to lift the wagon," George said.

The grumbling actors and actresses leaned on the branch. The wagon creaked and rose. George scurried to prop it up with several heavy crates. The company silently watched as he loosened the broken wheel with a hub nut wrench, which had been fastened to the wagon tongue. He struggled to secure the new wheel and tighten the hub again. He had seen Pa do the same countless times.

When it came time to reload the supplies, the actors and actresses did more complaining than actual work. George grunted as he carried box after box. His back ached from all the hauling and lifting. Pa would have been quick to point out that the wagon carried too much weight for Victor's starved, bony team. "Good feed and good rest," Pa always prescribed. George explained to Victor that the team had too much to haul.

"I appreciate your concern for dumb beasts," Victor said. "But I can't leave any of these costumes or scenery behind. How soon can you get us ready to leave?"

"As soon as the team is hitched up," George replied.

"Good work, George!" Victor replied, slapping him on the back. "Company! Get ready to roll out!"

The actors and actresses climbed into the wagon. "Get out of my seat!" Blanche shrieked at Estelle. "I am no mere chorus girl! I am the star in this two-bit operation!"

"Over my dead body!" replied Estelle, who refused

to budge from her place in the front of the wagon.

"Ladies, ladies!" Victor shouted. "This is not Italian opera. This is low burlesque of the worst possible kind. Now share the wagon space amiably or you will both walk!"

For the rest of the day, George followed the wagon on foot. He had been surprised to learn from Jacob that no one in the company was much of a shot. George borrowed the gun to hunt prairie chicken and grouse along the way. The game was plentiful. And he had no trouble catching up with the slow-moving wagon.

"Hail the returning hero!" Victor exclaimed when he saw George coming through the grass with five birds slung over his shoulder.

George smiled. Jacob whistled and applauded.

"I can't stand another mile in this bumpy wagon," Blanche complained. The rest of the company slumped on the ground, exhausted.

Victor agreed to camp nearby, even though they were far from wood or water. George had to walk nearly four miles to fill a bucket. It took Jacob nearly an hour to drag in enough branches to make a big fire.

George and Jacob plucked the birds and set them on a spit over the fire.

"Meat for dinner!" Horace said, smacking his lips.

The aroma of roasting prairie chickens filled the air.

George felt faint with hunger as he turned the spit. Jacob scraped what he could from the bottom of the flour barrel to make some thin pancakes, which he cooked on the griddle.

As darkness settled in, the actors and actresses huddled on the ground around the fire and ate quickly. For once, no one complained about George's smell. After dinner, Blanche sang a loud, happy tune. Then she lit a cigar and dealt four hands of poker.

"Play us a song, George," Victor said. He rested on the ground, studying his cards.

George willingly complied. He took out the trombone and played every waltz and dance melody he knew. The company applauded. "George, you are a talented individual. You will go far—mark my words!" Victor said. He raised his tin cup in the air. "To an excellent musician and an excellent cook!"

George smiled. "Jacob helped make dinner, too," he said modestly.

"Ah, but without your marksmanship, we never would have landed such toothsome birds. And without your skills, we never would have fixed the wagon so quickly," Victor said. "Hip-hip, hooray!"

"Hip-hip, hooray!" the other actors and actresses echoed.

George felt pleased by the attention. And it was pleasant

to have everyone in a cheerful mood—all except Jacob, who stared sullenly into the fire.

"To sleep!" Victor announced as soon as the poker game was finished. "Tomorrow is a busy day. We must cover much ground."

The company stretched and yawned. Since the night was cool, the actors and actresses unrolled blankets beside the fire. Exhausted but content, George drew his blanket around his shoulders and went to sleep with his head on his bag.

14 SOLO

The next day was bright and sunny. Since George was in charge of hunting and trapping food, he no longer had to worry about the horses or the wagon. Happily, he tramped along the ridges. He took time to watch a red-tailed hawk sail in a graceful circle overhead. It wasn't long before he had a brace of fine grouse and three prairie chickens. He knew Victor would be pleased.

When he finally caught up with the wagon, the company had stopped not far from a creek. After he had cleaned the prairie chickens and the fat grouse, he decided to wash his smelly jacket in the clear water. The stream wound its way through a fine stand of wolf willows. The bubbling water reminded him of Rattling Creek. He frowned; he did not want to think about home.

He splashed his face and his arms and rubbed behind his ears. The cool water felt wonderful on such a hot day. He dipped the green coat in the stream and watched it float lazily for a moment. He pushed it deeper and rubbed the sleeves together, hoping that might help get rid of the skunk smell. Mother's clean sheets hanging on the line were always so fragrant. He remembered running in the sunshine between the flapping sheets... remembered.... George rubbed the sleeves more briskly and thought instead about his trombone performance last night. How wonderful it had been to hear applause!

When he was through rinsing the coat, he hung it on a chokecherry bush to dry. He heard a splash. "Hello!" Victor called. He waded to the middle of the stream, dunked himself, and shook water from his hair the same way Buffalo shook water from his fur. "Wonderful!" he exclaimed, with a laugh as he climbed out. George laughed, too.

"Have a seat," Victor said, pointing to the bank. He and George sat down. Victor plucked a piece of grass and began to chew on one end. He spit out the grass and yodeled at the top of his lungs.

George jumped.

"Sorry to startle you," Victor said. "It's just that I've got such good news, I can't help myself."

George smiled. Pa only saw the worst that could happen. Not Victor. If he found something to be joyful about, he went right ahead and sang out. "What's the good news?" George asked.

"Jacob rode ahead after we set up camp. He wanted

to see what was up the road. And you'll never guess! He came upon four wagons full of reservation supplies. About a dozen soldiers are taking the wagons to the Rosebud Indian Agency. Best of all, the men have just been paid their wages."

George was confused. What was so wonderful about four wagons and some soldiers?

"This is our big opportunity," Victor continued. "After Jacob described our theatrical company in glowing detail, the soldiers invited us to perform for them tonight at their campsite."

"Tonight?"

"That's right. This is your chance, George. Your first solo in front of a real audience. We'll do a few comic dialogues, perhaps some ballads. Of course, nothing too morose. What I imagine is an operatic, spectacular, diabolic, musical, terpsichorean, farcical burletta." Victor jumped to his feet. "Come on! We've got to get the wagon on the road."

George did not completely understand what Victor was talking about, but he was swept away by the man's enthusiasm. "Will we put up the tent?" he asked excitedly. "Will we use scenery?"

"I'm afraid not," Victor said. "There just won't be time to set up for one of our formal performances. But we will be wonderful, I can assure you. We are professionals. The show must go on!"

"I was wondering...do you think I could wear one of those uniforms when I play my trombone?"

"Absolutely! And one other thing, George. I have an acting part for you in mind."

"An acting part?" George asked nervously.

"Well, it's not a classical role, really. More commercial than anything else. We need you to play the part of the poor lame boy when we demonstrate the power of Dr. Gregory's Wizard Oil. I think you can handle it just fine. Jacob will help you with a quick rehearsal or two." Victor patted George on the back. "It's a real honor, let me tell you. Without Wizard Oil we'd only have half the income we have today. The stuff's so powerful, I have to keep it under lock and key. Will you do it?"

George nodded eagerly. His first show!

"Go find Jacob. I think he's in the wagon," Victor said. "I'll go round up the others so we can begin packing."

George peeked between the canvas flaps. Jacob was inside, running his finger up and down the smooth brass of the trombone. "What are you doing?" George asked.

"Nothing," Jacob grumbled. "Where were you?"

"Down by the creek."

"With Victor?"

George nodded. "He told me the news. You did a great job finding an audience."

"Just in time. Did he mention we're out of food and nearly out of money? The way you've been using that gun, we'll be out of ammunition soon, too."

"If you want game to eat, I've got to use bullets." George felt his cheeks burn. "What's the matter?"

"Forget it," Jacob replied. He slipped the trombone back in the sack and handed it to George. "We're supposed to get the wagon loaded. We'd better get going."

George hesitated. He did not like to leave things between them so unpleasant. "I hope you don't mind having me for a student," he said lightly.

"What do you mean?"

"Victor said you're supposed to teach me how to play the part of the lame boy who's revived by Wizard Oil."

Instead of looking pleased, Jacob glowered even more darkly. "The lame boy's *my* role."

"Oh," George replied. Now he wished he had never been given the part. Why was Victor taking it away from Jacob?

"Come on," Jacob said gruffly. "I'll show you what to do."

Early that evening, the Barrett Theatre Company finally caught up with the soldiers. The four supply wagons were pulled into a circle under a grove of cottonwoods near Sand Creek. Mules were picketed in the tall grass not far away. With unlimited food—more than fifty government barrels of flour, salt pork, and canned goods—the soldiers seemed in no hurry to arrive at the Rosebud Agency. What was one more day on the road?

"Delighted to meet you!" announced Captain Little, a wiry, mustached man who stood in rapt attention as Blanche and Estelle descended from the wagon.

"Charmed, I'm sure!" twittered Blanche. Her voice had taken on a raspy, feminine quality George had never heard before. Could this be the same woman who had smoked a cigar and played a mean game of poker? Daintily, she held out her hand, gloved in white kidskin, for Captain Little. Not to be outdone, Estelle waved a lacy handkerchief. The captain kissed her hand, too. George rolled his eyes.

He had been surprised to learn that Victor expected him to play the role of the lame boy throughout the evening. Victor helped him down from the wagon, and George hobbled about on his crutches, trying to look pathetic.

Captain Little clicked his heels and bowed grandly. "We seldom get to see real theatre at the agency or at the fort. Will you join us for dinner? We have beef, beans, hardtack, and some promising-looking pudding."

"Certainly!" Victor replied. Without pausing to unpack, the company rushed to the soldiers' campfire and began helping themselves to the food. With great difficulty, George balanced his crutches and filled his plate. He shoveled the beans and meat into his mouth as fast as he could so that he could fill his plate again. When the meal was finished, Captain Little passed around a flask of whiskey. Dropping her ladylike image, Blanche wiped the neck of the flask with her sleeve, took a long swig, and belched.

"We will begin shortly," Victor said. Jacob nudged his father, who in turn signalled his actors and actresses to get on their feet. "Showtime!" he announced brightly. "If we sit and eat and drink too much longer, there won't *be* a performance."

Reluctantly, the company began unloading costumes and setting up a makeshift stage using several boxes and planks.

"What will you perform?" Captain Little asked Victor. "I'm very fond of *Uncle Tom's Cabin* and *Leah the Forsaken.* Are these part of your repertoire?"

"I'm afraid not," Victor replied. "But we have several pieces that I believe will appeal to an educated, sensitive man like yourself."

The soldiers sat down on kegs and boxes in a semi-circle around the stage area, which was lit with candles burning inside tin cans. He clapped his hands together. "Before we begin, I have a sad story to tell."

From somewhere behind the wagon, Estelle sang a mournful song. "You see," continued Victor, "we have a terrible tragedy here." He motioned to George, who hobbled between the candles and dragged himself up onto

163

the stage. "This young boy could run and walk like any other until the day he became lame."

George made a sorrowful face. Victor put his arm around his shoulder and whispered, "Cry."

George tried to squeeze out some tears, but nothing came.

"His parents dead, he came to us as an orphan, with no one in the world."

George made a more convincing sobbing noise. "A little louder," Victor hissed.

George howled.

"I have taken it upon myself to try and cure him since I discovered the magical properties of Dr. Gregory's Wizard Oil. This miraculous concoction, developed in the Far East, is the answer to lameness, muscle soreness, snakebite, horse bite, hair loss, lockjaw, deafness—"

"What about blindness?" one of the soldiers hooted.

"That, too," Victor said. He hissed in George's ear, "Ready?"

George moaned. He took a few faltering steps across the stage and rolled his eyes. He lunged forward, twisted into a terrible shape, and fell to the ground. The soldiers gasped.

"He's broken his neck!" Victor shouted, and leapt to George's side. George lay as if lifeless, his head back, his eyes staring crazily. "Keep back, fellows!" Victor pulled a bottle of Wizard Oil from his pocket and poured some into George's half-open mouth.

"George!" Victor whispered frantically. He shook him hard. "Come on! Come on, wake up!"

George's throat burned from swallowing great gulps of brown liquid, which smelled like fermented pig slop. He could hear Victor's voice. He could see his dimpled chin and the upside-down blue legs of the soldiers. But everything seemed very strange and far away. He felt as if he had walked outside himself and was looking at his own crumpled body lying there on the ground. Was this what Nellie had heard and seen before she went to heaven? He blinked back real tears.

"Look at that, folks! He's alive!" Victor shouted with relief. He poured some more Wizard Oil into George's mouth.

The crowd cheered. George felt himself being pulled to his feet. "There, you see!" Victor exclaimed loudly. "Wizard Oil works." He gave George a push. George walked. The soldiers whistled. "Only one dollar a bottle," cried Victor.

"Give me some!" a soldier called.

"Here's three silver dollars. I'll take three!"

Victor and Jacob were so busy selling bottles of Wizard Oil that they didn't notice George stumble off. Exhausted, he leaned against the wagon.

"Not a bad performance for an amateur," said Blanche. She was wearing a strange pink filmy outfit that made her look like an oversized butterfly. "Chin up. Here's your uniform. Remember, you're doing the opening fanfare, so make it good." She helped George into a jacket with gold braid, placed a hat on his head at a jaunty angle, and shoved the trombone into his hands. "Ready?"

George wiped his eyes with his sleeve and nodded. He felt numb as he returned to the stage. When he saw so many faces staring up at him in anticipation, he almost turned and ran.

"Go on, George. They're waiting for you!" Blanche hissed.

With trembling hands, George put the trombone to his lips. But then he forgot the sick feeling in the pit of his stomach; he played the fanfare better than he had ever played it while he was practicing. The notes soared into the night sky like a hundred red-tailed hawks. He no longer felt any fear. He was making music and people were listening to him. Really listening.

As soon as he finished, the soldiers cheered and clapped. George grinned and made an embarrassed bow. He stepped from the stage, dizzy and thrilled by his success.

"...forty-six, forty-seven, forty-eight, forty-nine," Victor said, counting out the silver dollars by the firelight.

The performance was over, and all the soldiers had retired for the night. The rest of the acting company had also gone to bed. Victor picked up the stacks of coins and tossed them inside a leather bag. "You did a wonderful job, George. Never seen blue coats dance like those fellows. Even after the show. I thought they'd never quit." Victor shook the bag. *Chink-chink-chink.*

George stared into the fire, pleased by Victor's praise.

"And you did a marvelous job with the lame-boy routine. Scared me for a moment there. I thought I'd really lost you," Victor said, chuckling. He stretched out his long legs by the crackling fire. Overhead the sky was filled with stars. "Yes, I'd say you have the makings of a really fine musician. Bet your family would have liked to have heard you play tonight."

George looked up in surprise. Victor had never asked about his family before.

"You're awfully generous, sir. You don't know anything about me, but you've let me come along with your company. I appreciate that. You see, I...I..." George cracked his knuckles. "I ran away from home. I hope you don't think that's too terrible, but that's what I did."

"Do you want to talk about it?"

George shook his head. He was quiet for several moments before he blurted, "You know, while I was lying there on the ground, I wasn't thinking about being a lame boy. I was thinking about my little sister. Her name was Nellie May. She died."

"When somebody close dies," Victor said gently, "it causes terrible pain."

Then without warning, the story rushed out. George told Victor everything he could remember about Nellie May—how she had looked and talked, and how she had died. "I should have watched her better," he mumbled. "I never told anyone. Not one soul. But it was all my fault she caught the measles." He talked about how he had disappointed his father his whole life, how he could never hope to please him, how unfeeling Pa was. "He's a tyrant. You see why I left home, don't you?" George begged, suddenly exhausted. "I had no choice."

Victor was silent for a long while. "Sounds like it was a difficult decision," he said at last. He poked the orange embers with a stick. Sparks flew. "When my wife died years ago, I blamed myself, too. She had tuberculosis. I bought her every kind of medicine I could find—every kind of cure. I just felt more and more helpless as she got worse." He paused and took a deep breath. "But there was nothing I could have done to save her. Nothing. It's taken me years to think this through."

Somehow sharing what he had been thinking all these long weeks made George feel relieved. "Does it ever go away?"

"What?"

"The pain."

Victor poked the embers again. "I'd be lying to you if I said you'll feel better in just a little while," he said slowly. "Have you ever cut your foot pretty bad?"

George nodded, remembering the time he accidentally injured his bare toe with a pitchfork. But what did that have to do with Nellie's death?

"How long did it take until you could run as fast as you used to?"

"Weeks, I guess," George replied. "I don't remember."

Victor rubbed his chin thoughtfully. "Grieving takes time, too. Sometimes the pain comes back when you least expect it—when Christmas comes around or maybe when you smell lilacs or hear a certain waltz. Just when you think you're getting better, all that yearning for the person you lost comes back again."

George's shoulders slumped. "You mean I'm never going to be rid of it?"

Victor shook his head. "In time you won't feel the pain the way you do now. Like the wound that healed, you'll be changed. The scar will always be there, but maybe you'll even be stronger. And one day you'll be able to run again. You just have to give yourself time."

George sighed. It all sounded much more difficult than he had thought it would be. But in some small way, he felt relieved. At last he had told someone who would listen, someone who was understanding. If only Victor were his father! If only—

"Hello, there!" Jacob called as he crept out of the nearby bushes. He appeared so abruptly, George wondered how long he had been listening to their conversation. "The work's finished, Victor," he said, smiling. "I filled the bags with sand and the boxes with rocks."

George didn't know what Jacob was talking about, but he was too embarrassed to ask.

"Good work!" Victor said. "Now it's time for you boys to turn in. We leave before dawn."

George struggled to his feet. He unrolled his blanket beside the fire. As he did, he saw Jacob watching him. He gave George a withering look and then turned away. A chill ran down George's spine.

15 WIZARD OIL
AND THE U.S.G.

The next morning before dawn, the theatre company packed all the costumes and scenery. Although their campsite was located some distance from the soldiers' supply wagons, the actors and actresses took remarkable care not to wake their sleeping hosts.

George had never seen such speed or heard so little complaining. "Aren't we even going to say goodbye?" he asked Horace, who sat beside him in the back of the wagon.

"Keep your voice down," Horace murmured. "Wizard Oil doesn't work indefinitely, you know."

Blanche winked at George. "Those soldier boys need their rest. They're heading south today along Dog Ear's Creek. I know. Captain Little told me they're going to try and make forty miles before Sunday."

"Good speed to 'em," Horace said, and then chuckled. "By the time they get to the Rosebud, I bet they'll regret letting their guards take medicine on duty."

Blanche giggled.

George smiled, pretending he understood the joke, too. But as the wagon bumped and lurched along, George watched the soldiers' camp in the distance, and his grin vanished. Why wasn't anyone waking up and starting a cooking fire? He squinted but he saw no movement. What was wrong?

A warm wind chanted across the prairie, whistling and hissing among the stands of buffalo grass and prickly pear. Tumbleweed dashed across the road. Little by little, the sky began to brighten. It was going to be a hot day.

"I'm hungry," Blanche complained.

"You're always hungry," Horace said. He reached inside a canvas sack marked "U.S.G." and pulled out a handful of hardtack. He tossed the crackers to everyone in the wagon. "Eat hearty, compliments of Uncle Sam."

The actors and actresses laughed. As George nibbled the hardtack, he noticed five more bags marked "U.S.G." hidden beneath the crates of Wizard Oil. They had not been there before. "What's 'U.S.G.'?" George asked.

"Did you ever hear such a stupid boy?" Blanche laughed. She tugged a gold watch from inside her sleeve and swung it on its chain. "Ever hear of the United States Government?"

Horace's eyes narrowed. "Put that away," he ordered.

172

"You're going to ruin everything again, aren't you?"

Blanche tucked the watch back in its hiding place. "I am not," she said, pouting.

Horace jerked his thumb toward the front of the wagon and asked in a low voice, "Does Victor know?"

"Why should he care?"

"You little fool," Estelle grumbled. "You'll land us all in jail again, won't you?"

"J-jail?" George said. "You've been to jail?"

Steele shrugged. "Let's just say that not every town we visit treats us with the respect we deserve."

George had never known anyone who had been in jail. He had always assumed that hardened criminals were the only ones locked up behind bars. Were Blanche and the others hardened criminals? What awful things had they done? Since he was part of the theatre company now, would he be considered guilty, too? What would it be like to be locked away the rest of his life? There was Mother, come to visit on Christmas Day and her eyes red from crying. And George, so guilty, so hopeless...

"Nobody never proved nothing against me in Vermillion," Blanche insisted. "I was innocent."

Horace snorted disagreeably. "You never learn. As soon as Captain Little notices his watch is gone, they'll be after us. It won't take him long then to figure out the food is missing."

Blanche shrank against the side of the wagon. Horace leapt to the ground. "Victor!" he called.

"What's the matter now?" Victor asked, pulling the horses to a halt. Horace climbed up on the wagon seat beside Victor and Jacob. George could not hear their conversation, but he could tell that Victor was upset. His face was growing redder by the minute.

He shook the reins and drove the wagon off the road. "What's happening?" Estelle demanded. "All this bumping's jarring my hairdo!"

Victor did not reply. He drove on until they reached the protection of a grove of trees near a small creek, where he finally stopped. "Everyone out," he ordered.

"What's going on?" Estelle said angrily. "You said we were going to make fifteen miles today."

"Well, we've had a change in plans," Victor said. He gave Blanche an angry glare. "I need to study the map to come up with a new route. In the meantime, why don't you eat some government grub. It's slowing us down. Horace, start a fire so Jacob can fry some pancakes."

Jacob hurried to retrieve the griddle and costume barrel, which now contained twenty pounds of flour. As soon as Horace and Steele had gotten a small fire going, he began to fry pieces of salt pork. Then he mixed up the pancake batter.

Victor pulled out a map and unfolded it. "George?"

174

he called. "I want to ask you something. Have you ever heard of another way to get to Deadwood?"

Helplessly, George tried to focus on the map. He wanted to believe that Victor had not been responsible for the stolen food. What was it Jacob had said last night about bags filled with sand and boxes loaded with rocks? Of course Victor had known. He had known all along. Stealing food had been part of the plan. "The wagon road's the only way I've heard of," George said slowly.

"There must be some other route across," Victor insisted.

"We could follow the White River for a while," George said, pointing at the twisting line that ran east and west. "Only problem is that we'll be trespassing—going right through Indian territory. That could be asking for trouble."

"No worse than what we're in right now," Victor said. "We've got to stay off the main road for a while in case soldiers come looking for us. Don't look so glum, George. They might not even notice anything's missing before we reach the Black Hills. But I don't want to take any chances."

George felt more and more uneasy. There was so much uncertainty and danger around him. He did not like the idea of prison or being chased by soldiers. It had been wrong to steal the food and the watch. And it was wrong to run away like this. He wished he were far away from here—safe and secure in his own house, in his own bed.

"Players!" Victor said. "As soon as you finish your meal, we will be on our way. George has provided us with an excellent suggestion."

"What's that?" Jacob asked in a surly voice.

"To elude any possibility of capture, we are going to follow the White River for the next few miles," Victor explained. "When all danger is past, we'll return to the main road."

"I don't like this idea," Estelle complained.

Blanche nodded. "What if we get lost?"

"Or scalped," Steele said.

"Angels and ministers of grace defend us!" Estelle said, and gasped. Her hands flew to her stiff, blonde curls.

Horace pointed to George. "And why should we listen to him? He's brought us bad luck before—"

"I will not listen to another word," Victor interrupted. "We're wasting time. Now let's pack up."

George and Jacob walked to lighten the load so the horses could move more rapidly. Jacob strode on ahead, walking stick in hand. George stayed by the wagon. A row of dark clouds had come up on the horizon, and George felt the wind shift. "Looks like rain!" he called to Victor.

All of a sudden, there was a flash of lightning. One of the horses reared with a terrified whinny. The harness snapped, and the animal bolted away at full gallop.

176

"Stop that beast!" Victor cried. Horace, Steele, and Jacob ran after the spooked horse while Estelle and Blanche stood beside the wagon shrieking and waving their skirts. The horse dodged around Horace and thundered past Jacob. When it slowed, Jacob hollered and made a dramatic lunge, but the horse bucked and fled before he could grab the dangling reins.

George watched in disgust. Pa had taught him that the best way to catch a frightened horse was to walk up slow and easy and talk softly. Didn't they realize that all their commotion was only going to frighten the poor creature more? They had to get that horse back. Without it, how would they escape from the soldiers? George would have to trail the horse himself. That wasn't going to be easy now that a storm was coming up and—

"Help!" Jacob's voice rang out. Ahead of George, he fell to his knees and disappeared in the tall grass.

16 A TERRIFYING POSSIBILITY

"Jacob!" George cried, hurrying toward him. "Jacob!" But there was no answer. The air vibrated with the sound of clicking dry bones.

Only a few feet away lay coiled the biggest rattlesnake George had ever seen. Its brown and tan markings blended so well with the surrounding muddy ground and grass that the three-foot-long rattler was almost invisible. George's palms began to sweat. His stomach twisted into a hard knot. He watched the angry snake raise its head.

"Over here," Jacob moaned. "Something bit me. My ankle, it's burning..." He lay curled on the ground with his knee pressed to his chest and his face contorted in pain.

"Don't move," George said softly. What should he do? The snake could strike again. He clenched and unclenched his empty fists. If only he had a rock! The rattler's bold, black eyes glittered. Its delicate tongue flashed once, twice, taunting George. Then, like a ghost, it slithered away.

George took a small step forward. He knew the unwritten law. See a snake, kill it. But he had let this one escape. Now he faced the terrifying possibility that it might still be close by, waiting for him.

"George!"

Still, George did not move. He saw snakes everywhere— slithering around his feet, curling around rocks and clumps of grass. He put his hands to his ears to block the buzzing, rasping roar of a hundred snakes, all calling, *Death comesssssssssss!*

"Aren't you going to help me?" Jacob cried, louder this time.

George blinked. The snakes vanished. He took his hands from his ears. Now all that he heard was Jacob's whimpering. All that he saw was Jacob writhing on the ground. If only Pa were here; he would know what to do. Pa would know how to save Jacob.

George took a deep breath. He had to find a way. He had to do it alone.

"I'm coming, Jacob." George jammed his hand into his pocket and pulled out Shy's knife. With one swift movement, he cut and ripped a strip of cloth from the bottom of his own shirt. "Hold still," he said, kneeling. He tied the cloth tightly below Jacob's knee. He had seen his father do the same thing to a snakebit cow whose leg had swelled to twice its normal size. The cow had spent the rest of the day chest-deep in creek mud and seemed no worse off from the experience. Would the same treatment work on a human?

Jacob's ankle was beginning to puff around two bloody fang marks. The skin was taking on a bruised purple color. Was the poison spreading?

George grabbed a handful of mud. "What are you doing, smearing mud all over my leg?" Jacob demanded.

"Sucks out snake venom," George said with as much authority as he could muster. He dug up huge handfuls and covered Jacob's ankle.

"What's going on here?" Horace asked, out of breath.

"Rattler just bit Jacob," George said.

Horace's jaw dropped. He pulled out a flask and took a long swig. "Just a preventative," he explained, then handed the flask to Jacob. "Here. This is the best snakebite medicine I know. Take a good swallow."

Jacob took a sip and made a face.

Horace called to the others, who came running to see what had happened.

"Jacob!" Victor said. His face was pale and his hands were shaking. "What should we do? What should we do?"

"I know a good cure," Estelle announced. "Kill a rooster. Put the warm body on the wound. When the bird turns black from the snake poison, slap on another."

Jacob screamed in pain.

"Where we going to get a rooster all the way out here?" Blanche asked.

"I think George has things pretty well under control," Horace said. "What do you need, George?"

"Water. I'm making a mud plaster."

"I'll go back to the wagon and get the canteen," Horace volunteered. "I'm afraid I don't have much of a bedside manner."

"There's one snakebite cure that works every time. It's a chant," Blanche said. "We sprinkle cold water on Jacob's face. Then we shout three times, 'Get up. It is the command of T.C. Ramachauder Rao.' "

"Who is T.C. Ramachauder Rao?" Estelle asked.

Blanche shrugged. "Somebody who invented the cure. Say, if you don't believe me, why don't we try some Wizard Oil? That's supposed to work. We got a whole wagon full. Won't hurt to use a bottle. What do you say, Boss?"

Victor knelt beside his son, too preoccupied to reply. Blanche hurried off. When she returned, she poured a little Wizard Oil into Jacob's mouth. He gagged and spit most of it out.

When Horace returned with water, he splashed some into the dirt. George made a fresh mud slab and patted it gently on Jacob's leg. "We're going to need more water."

"I'll go down to the creek," Horace said. "You sure this cure works?"

"I'm sure," George said confidently, though he really wasn't sure at all. He had often observed his father tending a neighbor's ailing animal. No matter how desperate the situation, Pa would never admit that he might not know exactly what he was doing. George decided he'd follow the same tactic. "We need mud!" he ordered. The actors and actresses scurried about to mix more dirt with water.

Rain was beginning to splatter the ground. Jacob groaned. George tried to make him more comfortable by folding Keturah's coat beneath his head. "It's too dangerous to move Jacob into the wagon," he told Horace and Steele. "Can you rig up some kind of protection and then move the wagon closer?"

Horace nodded. He and Steele found some branches and an extra piece of canvas to create a makeshift tent over Jacob, who was now vomiting repeatedly. The actors and actresses pushed and pulled the wagon near the spot where Jacob lay. Not once did Victor leave his son's side. He seemed incapable of making any decisions, giving any directions.

"I'm cold," Estelle complained beneath the dripping wagon.

"We could make a fire if we could get enough dry wood together," Horace suggested. "Steele, are you coming with me?"

"All right," Steele replied, reluctantly. He found his

umbrella in the wagon, opened it, and followed Horace and the remaining horse in the direction of a grove of trees. In a little while they returned with a load of firewood. But the rain came down harder than ever. Since it was impossible to start a fire, the wood was dragged underneath the wagon to keep dry.

George watched Jacob anxiously. He seemed to be getting weaker. Twice he told George his face felt strangely numb.

"Is he...is he going to get better?" Victor whispered. George nodded.

"Angels and ministers of grace defend us!" Victor mumbled.

"Why don't you get some sleep? I'll watch him."

"I'm unbelievably tired," Victor admitted. "Just let me sleep a half hour. Then I'll watch him." He rested his head on a box of Wizard Oil beneath the makeshift tent.

It was a long night. Jacob finally stopped vomiting and drifted off to sleep. George continued to apply fresh mud to his ankle. The rest of the actors and actresses huddled beneath the wagon. Like George, they too listened for the sound of soldiers' horses.

In the morning the sky cleared. Wet clothes were hung on the wagon. While Horace kept watch in the direction of the road, Steele managed to start a fire. George acted as cook. For the first time in weeks, the company had hot coffee to drink and cornmeal gruel that wasn't scorched.

When George brought Jacob his breakfast, he was shocked to see him sitting up. "George, when you going to let me get out of this mess?" Jacob demanded. "I got a terrible cramp in my knee."

George laughed, filled with relief. He knew his cure must be working if Jacob had energy enough to complain.

As his son's health improved, so did Victor's spirits. "Our luck is returning! And see who's come to visit," he exclaimed as the runaway horse wandered into camp.

"I bet those soldiers aren't even on our trail," Estelle said. "What I want to know is when are we going to get moving?"

"Tomorrow," Victor replied. "I think Jacob will be well enough to ride then. Don't you, George?"

George nodded. But throughout the day, he kept Jacob under careful watch. He gave him hot tea to drink and did not allow him to move his leg.

"I'm tired of lying here like this!" Jacob complained. "This mud makes me itch. Let me up!" But George refused.

By nightfall the rest of the company had become restless, too. They drank several bottles of Wizard Oil and sang around the fire.

"Why don't you play for us, George?" Estelle said.

"Come on," Blanche coaxed. "Be a good fellow."

George played his trombone. But when he was finished, the applause did not delight him the way it once had. He felt sad, and he did not know why. After Jacob was settled as comfortably as possible and the rest of the company had finally dropped off to sleep, George lay against his burlap sack. He stared up at the moon.

At this very moment, was someone at Oak Hollow gazing at the moon, too?

"George!" Jacob whispered.

George crawled closer. "What's the matter? Your ankle hurting bad?"

Jacob shook his head. "I feel much better. Here, I got something for you." He reached inside his shirt pocket and pressed something into George's hand.

In the flickering firelight, George counted ten silver dollars. "This is Wizard Oil money. Why are you giving it to me?" he asked.

"I owe you."

"Why? That snakebite—"

"You don't understand," Jacob interrupted. "This money isn't for the snakebite cure. It's for the road."

"The road?"

Jacob glanced around uneasily. "You've got to get out of here," he whispered. "Tonight."

George squirmed. "What are you talking about?"

"Horace and the others...their minds are made up that

you're a Jonah—that you've brought us bad luck. I know it's ridiculous, but they blame everything that's gone wrong on you. That's why they're planning to get rid of you tomorrow. There'll be a little accident, and nobody'll ever suspect."

"Tomorrow? An accident?"

"Let me finish. There's not much time. After they get rid of you, they're going to take your trombone. They plan to sell it in Deadwood."

George's face flushed with anger. He would never let them take his trombone. Never! "Does Victor know?"

Jacob shook his head. "He doesn't suspect anything."

"Then how come you know so much?"

Jacob sighed. "I was the one who originally thought of the idea."

"You!" George felt as if someone had just knocked all the air out of him.

"Let me explain," Jacob whispered anxiously. "I'll admit it was my idea. I didn't like all the attention you've been getting. And we needed the money. I thought we could just give you a rap on the head that would leave you unconscious long enough for us to make our escape. But now I can't go through with it. How could I? I owe you my life. That's why I'm warning you. You've got to get out of here."

George sat silently, the cool metal of the silver dollars

pressed in his hand. They reminded him of something. A gold pocket watch he had once held in a dream—the dream he'd had when he'd been sick with the measles. The dream with his father's face in it.

"George, you better get packing."

Jacob's voice made George jump. He smoothed Keturah's jacket and rolled it inside the blanket. He took a canteen, some matches, and some hardtack, and he wrapped a piece of salt pork in his handkerchief. He slung the burlap sack over his shoulder. The night was clear and mild; there was a full moon. He could make ten miles before sunup.

One last time he looked around the camp. He wished he could say goodbye to Victor. He wished he could thank him for all that he had told him.

"Safe journey!" Jacob whispered.

George smiled and waved. Jacob called softly, "Where you headed?"

"Home," George replied.

17 A SONG FOR NELLIE

After two days of walking, George recrossed the Missouri River. He bid farewell to Keturah and spent all but one silver dollar and a fifty cent piece on a train ticket. The ride from Chamberlain to Marion to Defiance was dusty and uneventful. Not until he began walking the five miles from Defiance to Oak Hollow did his excited anticipation unravel into nervous fear.

How would he explain his disappearance? Would Mother and Pa believe him? And what about Addie and Lew and Burt? Maybe they hated him for the sorrow and worry he had caused them. Worse yet, what if they hadn't even missed him?

Wind hissed. Grasshoppers jumped out from underfoot as he walked. Flies hummed, and blackbirds called out a raucous welcome. He had never noticed before the way the Oak Hollow landscape danced with light. How pale and silver the unfurling corn leaves looked! Homesickness flooded his senses.

Overhead, cloud fingers beckoned. The whole sky seemed to breathe down on him like a challenge—like a laughing promise-maker. Who did he think he was?

George scanned the next rise. Beyond that was his family's soddy. What was he going to say the minute he saw everyone? How should he act?

He felt foolish and afraid. And yet he knew there was no turning back. For courage, he put his trombone to his lips and played. His melody was about flight and mischief and a stubborn spirit. It was a song for Nellie May.

Somewhere close by a dog barked. Then a familiar black shape bounded through the tall grass.

"Buffalo!" George shouted joyfully. The big dog jumped, slobbered, and nearly knocked him over.

"George?" a voice called out.

George turned and saw Pa running toward him across the field. Pa's arms were outstretched. He swept up George, trombone and all. "It's really you," he said, his voice shaking. His eyes hungrily searched George's face. "You've come back."

How could George tell his father about his journey? He could say that he'd had an adventure—that he'd visited a faraway place and survived on his own and played his

music before a real audience. How could he talk about Nellie and say that he was afraid what had happened was somehow his fault?

Just now, George did not mention any of these things. Instead, he hugged his father as hard as he could. When he stepped back, to his amazement, he saw tears streaming down Pa's cheeks.

The lump in George's throat was so large that he thought he'd never be able to swallow again.

Pa wiped his eyes quickly. He coughed. "Barbed-wire fence went down," he said.

George gripped his trombone. Was Pa going to lecture him about missed chores? "I was doing repairs," Pa continued, "and Buffalo and I heard you playing. What's the name of that tune?"

"Doesn't have a name exactly. Came out of my head. I just made it up. Kind of reminds me of Nellie."

Pa rubbed his chin. "Reminds me of Nellie, too. You'll play it again some time, won't you?"

"Sure, Pa," George said. He sighed with relief. Then he smiled and slung the sack with the trombone over his shoulder. "Let's go home."

About the Author

LAURIE LAWLOR began creating the characters of the Mills family while unraveling Dakota homesteading stories told by her mother and grandmother. What began as an investigation of family folklore ended in a two-year research project that ultimately took Ms. Lawlor back to South Dakota to the actual site of her great-grandparents' farm. Hundred-year-old photographs, letters, diaries, oral histories, census records, newspaper accounts, deeds, and reminiscences were all part of the material she used in *Addie Across the Prairie, Addie's Dakota Winter, Addie's Long Summer,* and *George on His Own.*

Laurie Lawlor teaches as well as writes. She lives with her husband and two children in Evanston, Illinois.